HEARTSIDE BAY

THE **HEARTSIDE BAY** SERIES

HEARTSIDE BAY

The New Girl

CATHY COLE

SCHOLASTIC

First published in 2014 by Scholastic Children's Books
An imprint of Scholastic Ltd
Euston House, 24 Eversholt Street, London, NW1 1DB, UK
Registered office: Westfield Road, Southam, Warwickshire, CV47 0RA
SCHOLASTIC and associated logos are trademarks and/or
registered trademarks of Scholastic Inc.

ISBN 978 1407 14046 9

A CIP catalogue record for this book
is available from the British Library.

Printed by CPI Group (UK) Ltd, Croydon, CR0 4YY
Papers used by Scholastic Children's Books are made
from wood grown in sustainable forests.

1 3 5 7 9 10 8 6 4 2

This is a work of fiction. Names, characters, places, incidents
and dialogues are products of the author's imagination or are used
fictitiously. Any resemblance to actual people, living or dead,
events or locales is entirely coincidental.

www.scholastic.co.uk

With special thanks to Lucy Courtenay
and Sara Grant

ONE

"Mum?" Lila Murray began hesitantly.

Her mum looked up from the half unpacked box on the kitchen table. "Hmm?"

Now it came down to it, Lila couldn't speak.

You've practised this, she told herself. *Just put it out there!*

She had gone over the words she would use as she got out of her bed in the unfamiliar house and felt the hard floorboards under her feet. She had repeated them stubbornly to herself as she brushed her glossy shoulder-length brown hair and tried to fix it into some kind of style that didn't shout "troublemaker" the way it always had back in London. She had rehearsed them in her head as she wiped off the thick rim of eyeliner she had put on and switched instead for a light flick of mascara to frame her big blue eyes, and straightened her tie so it actually met the button on her shirt collar for once, and resisted the urge to roll her skirt up. Why couldn't she say them now? Was it because they made everything too . . . real?

"I want to be called Lila in Heartside Bay," she said in a tumble. "Not Lil. If I'm ever going to settle in around here, I have to start again. It's time for me to be someone else."

She lifted her chin, challenging her mother to say something. Her mum was a psychotherapist, and tended to ask gentle questions that made people open up and bawl out their problems. Lila hoped she was strong enough to stick it out in the face of her mum's questions and sympathy.

"That's nice," said her mum. "It makes me think of flowers. Lilacs, and lilies."

That was it? Lila couldn't believe her luck.

"See you," she said, backing out of the house with her schoolbag on her shoulder.

Flowers were good, Lila told herself firmly, heading

down the path and on to the street. Flowers marked out someone who didn't go round wrecking lives and falling in love with the wrong people. She'd done too much of that already.

It was pretty bad, moving to the love capital of Britain a week before Valentine's Day. Everything here was so perfect and neat and happy, the complete opposite of how broken and messy Lila felt. Even with her toned down make-up and her neat, regulation uniform, would she ever fit in here? As she walked, all she could see were perfect little houses, matching front doors, gum-free pavements and brightly coloured window boxes. And hearts. Hearts *everywhere*. The wrought-iron lampposts, metal dustbins, even the manhole covers were covered in hearts. Like she needed reminding about love!

She turned her face to the fresh breeze blowing in from the sea. From up here by the cliffs, the famous heart shape of Heartside Bay was clearly visible, with a sweeping pier forming one arm of the heart and a natural outcropping of rocks forming the other. It looked more like a bum than a heart, Lila decided.

She corrected herself. *Lil* would have thought it looked like a bum. *Lila* would think it was cute. Lila would be taken seriously around here. Lila would get it right.

Her phone vibrated. She glanced at the screen.

Miss u. Call me xx

She ignored it without responding. Then, absent-mindedly tracing the S and G hidden in the little swirling heart tattoo on her wrist, she sped up. Her mum had offered her a lift. She wished she'd accepted. A sweaty hairline was not the best way to make a first impression.

Schoolkids were flowing down the high street in packs. The Valentine's Day banners on the buildings, the strings of heart-shaped lights above her head and the pink-painted tarmac beneath her feet made Lila feel dizzy. Trying to ignore the tinny sound of love songs blasting through the town speakers, she jogged after them.

The beginning of a nervous headache was starting behind her eyes as she caught her breath on the steps of

Heartside High. A bell started ringing deep inside the big white building. Running up the steps in a flash of panic, Lila looked down to give her blazer sleeve a tug to cover her tattoo.

She crashed into something hard.

"Whoa!"

A warm arm grabbed her. Grabbing it back, Lila managed to stop herself from falling backwards down the steps.

"Holding hands with me already? Whatever happened to 'I'll call you'?"

Flustered, Lila dropped the hand and straightened her tie. She couldn't believe she'd been so clumsy. "Sorry. First day. You know?" She gestured vaguely. "Steps. Bad id—"

She looked up. Her rescuer was tall and broad, his blond hair shiny and dishevelled. Without thinking, she scanned him. Tie undone at the neck, lightly tanned skin. He was hot.

He raised his eyebrows. "Like what you see?"

Lila could feel her face turning pink. It always betrayed her like this. She hated her pale skin. She would have to work extra-hard at hiding all the feelings she used to show to the world without caring.

"I need to find, uh. . ." She rummaged in her bag and pulled out a piece of paper. "10Y?"

"That's my class," he said. "We have English first thing with Mr Morrison, our class tutor. I'll take you in if you like. I'm Ollie."

"Lil. I mean, Lila."

A second bell went. He was looking at her in that lazy kind of way that made her stomach flutter.

"Shouldn't we, you know. . . ?" She waved at the double doors. "Go inside?"

What was wrong with her? He would think she had half a brain, but she couldn't help it. Every time she looked into his deep blue eyes, she lost her ability to speak in full sentences.

"You're new. You can be as late as you like."

"But what about you?"

"I'm helping you," he pointed out, as they walked towards the office. "Right?"

The receptionist gave Lila an armful of paper and a map. Without thinking, she pushed up her sleeves to get a better grip.

"Nice tat," Ollie remarked.

Lila almost dropped everything. He'd got up quite close to her ear without her noticing.

"I . . . thanks." She cursed her idiocy. Lil was already making her presence felt. Now Ollie would think of her as the girl with the stupid tattoo.

Ollie set off at a light jog. "Let's find your locker first. You can dump some of your stuff."

Everywhere people were flitting into classrooms, laughter cut short as doors slammed shut. Several people looked curiously at Lila. She was half glad to be walking with someone – especially a hot guy – and half wishing the floor would open up beneath her. She felt ridiculous in a uniform, which she'd never had to wear before. Her hair had a kink in the side, which she normally dealt with by tousling up her whole head. She could feel it sticking out sideways. She wanted to fling open her arms and shout: "This isn't me!" But it *was* her. It *had* to be her.

"So," said Ollie. "This is it. The dump. The joint. The state penitentiary."

Heartside High didn't look like any of those things. It was bright, light, modern and strangely clean. Lila, who was more used to graffiti on classroom doors and kicked-in lockers than polished concrete floors and hung artwork in stairwells, found it impressive.

"Just moved to Heartside?" Ollie asked as they found Lila's locker in the Year 10 corridor.

She put a few things away, then shifted her armful of paper to a more comfortable spot. "We moved from London last week. My parents have new jobs here."

She wondered if he would ask for details. What would she say if he did? There would be way too much explaining to do, and she wasn't feeling up to it.

But to her relief, he didn't ask any questions. He pointed at a room they were passing. "Staffroom. Avoid unless someone's dared you to put washing-up liquid in the coffee machine."

Lila laughed, starting to relax. "You've done that?"

He grinned. "How did you guess?"

They headed up some steps, past a gleaming trophy cabinet stuffed with cups and brightly polished dishes. A tall guy in a tracksuit came out of a room beside the trophies. He looked at Ollie with narrowed eyes.

"If you've come to tell me you can't make practice today, Wright, you're on the bench this weekend," he began. "I don't give a pig's butt if—" He noticed Lila. "Who are you?"

"Lila Murray." Her new name still felt weird. "I'm new."

"And I'm showing her to class," Ollie put in.

"10Y is that way, last time I looked," said the teacher. He pointed back down the corridor.

"Short cut," Ollie said with an innocent shrug.

Lila's gaze was snagged by the name inscribed on the base of a small silver football trophy directly in her eyeline. OLIVER WRIGHT.

"Is that you?" she asked, peering at it more closely.

"Top scorer last season," he said casually. "See you later, sir."

"I'm watching you, Wright," the teacher called after them.

It was obvious that Ollie had brought Lila this way to show her his trophy. She fought down the reckless feeling rising inside her. She wondered what he would do if she put her arms round him and kissed him on the spot. Lil would have done it in a heartbeat, but Lila didn't want to spend too much time thinking about boys, however cute they were. But where was the harm in a little flirting?

"I liked your trophy," she said, glancing up at him through her lashes.

His teeth flashed into a wide smile. "Did you?"

She suddenly felt uncertain. Was this Lila flirting, or Lil?

"10Y?" she said, with a sudden briskness in her voice.

Ollie was big into football. Lila let him talk as they walked down the white corridor.

". . .so we beat these schools from all over this area. Actually, it's probably more accurate to say we whipped them. Seven-nil in one match. Five goals scored by me. But you know, obviously, it's a team game, so the guys get all the credit. Most of the credit. Some of the credit."

"Wow," said Lila as they reached a classroom door marked 10Y: MR MORRISON, ENGLISH. "I feel like we just found the source of the Amazon."

"You're funny," Ollie said admiringly, leaning against the door above her head. "Funny and—"

And then, like in some kind of horror movie, the door swung open and deposited them both on the classroom floor, Ollie on top.

TWO

The room erupted. A tall man with his hands on his hips and a pair of glasses balanced on top of his head looked down at Lila in astonishment. Mr Morrison, she guessed from the depths of her mortification. From her angle on the floor, he looked as high as a mountain.

"Lila Murray, I presume?" he enquired amid a storm of catcalling and applause.

Lila struggled upright, shoving Ollie away from her. Her face was completely aflame. Could there have been a worse way to make an entrance? "Sorry I'm late," she stammered.

"These corridors can be distracting."

Lila had never heard so few words from a teacher sound quite so withering. Laughing his head off, Ollie bowed to the whistling still coming from the back of the room.

"Sit," Mr Morrison said to Ollie, as if he were talking to a disobedient dog. "Miss Murray, sit at the back beside Miss Nelson."

As Ollie sauntered to his seat, high-fiving as he went, Lila cringed a hundred times over. She wanted to bury her head. Everyone was looking at her, talking about her and pointing at her. One boy in glasses was staring so hard that she wondered if his eyes would leave some kind of imprint on her skin. So much for blending in. Now she had what amounted to a big neon arrow over her head, flashing "TOTAL SCREW-UP".

One girl in particular, who was seated near the front, seemed to be giving Lila the evil eye. Even in the hideous black and red Heartside uniform, she looked like some kind of supermodel. She was slim and long-legged, and her red hair fell halfway down her back in the kind of sleek waves seen on hairspray ads. An expensive silver watch peeped out from under her shirt cuff. Her skin was flawless and her eyes were a clear blue-grey. Lila felt them hammering into her like two steel nails.

"Nice watch," she mumbled, for want of anything better to say.

"Going to steal that as well?" the supermodel enquired.

Lila felt extra-mortified. This girl was obviously going out with Ollie. Lila couldn't help but feel a stab of disappointment.

Mr Morrison handed Lila a worksheet. "Enough chit-chat, ladies. Off you go, Miss Murray."

Lila kept her eyes on the floor as she walked through the classroom and sank into the spare desk beside a girl with a blunt blue-black fringe and a pair of quirky zigzag earrings.

"Don't mind Eve the Ice Queen," said the girl. She had a light American accent. "She's well known for keeping her soul in the deep freeze. I'm Polly. Welcome to Heartside High."

"Hi, thanks," Lila said, grateful for a friendly face. "Sorry about the entrance. It wasn't exactly planned. And it wasn't what it looked like."

"Ollie Wright isn't known for his subtlety."

Lila spent a couple of minutes hunting down a pencil, thankful for something to take her mind off her embarrassment. When she cautiously emerged from the depths of her bag, she was relieved to see that most of the class had lost interest in her. Bending her head, she tackled the worksheet. It could have been written in hieroglyphics, for all the sense she made of it. Her mind whirred through everything she'd learned already that morning.

Ollie: hot football-playing show-off. Polly: friendly American with interesting jewellery. Eve: beautiful witch with a wand already positioned between Lila's shoulder blades. Ollie and Eve: clearly together. *Only another twenty-three people to get to know. . .*

She scanned the rest of the room. The staring boy in glasses had bent his head so close to the desk she wondered if he had fallen asleep. Avoiding stares from a few of the boys looking a little too knowingly in her direction as well as a wink from Ollie, her eyes slowed to a halt.

No way, thought Lila, astonished and more than a little freaked out. *Make that twenty-two.*

Rhiannon Wills' distinctive curly hair was bent towards Eve the Ice Queen. They were deep in conversation. How had Lila not noticed her at the start? More to the point, how had *Rhi* not noticed *Lila*?

She felt uncomfortable as she thought about the last time she and Rhi had met. It hadn't been Lil's finest hour. They hadn't seen each other for a couple of years now. Maybe Rhi hadn't recognized her new look, or her new name. Maybe Rhi didn't *want* to recognize her. Or maybe it wasn't Rhi at all, she thought hopefully.

"Who's the girl next to Eve?" she asked Polly in a low voice.

"That's Rhi," said Polly, confirming Lila's fears. "She and Eve are best buddies."

"Is Eve going out with Ollie?" Lila asked, desperate to know.

Ollie was just a stupid jock, she tried to tell herself. A jock who'd made sure Lila Murray was notorious before her first lesson had even begun. It wasn't like she was seriously interested in him or anything – was she?

"She wishes," Polly said. "But if you believe what Eve tells you, it's only a matter of time. She's queen bee of Heartside, you see. What could be more natural than dating the school's football star? It's destiny." She smirked.

Mr Morrison clapped his hands. "OK, you've had enough time with those worksheets. Themes in *Of Mice and Men* by John Steinbeck. Who's going to start us off?"

Polly put up her hand. "Friendship, sir."

"Thank you, Miss Nelson." Mr Morrison's gaze settled on Polly's earrings. "And lose the jewellery. The rules of Heartside are clear: studs only."

Polly flushed. She slowly removed her earrings and tucked them into her pocket before adding in a low voice to Lila: "Of course, Eve wouldn't know real friendship if it bit her on her designer-clad butt. That's the trouble with growing up rich and spoilt. You think the world owes you everything."

Lila was surprised by the venom in Polly's voice. If Eve was so bad, she wondered what Rhi saw in her. Rhi was a decent person, at least back when she'd known her. She didn't deserve the way Lil had treated her.

"One to avoid, then," she said.

Polly nodded. "When Eve Somerstown marks your card, you know about it," she said a little bitterly.

Lila wondered when and how Eve had marked Polly's.

She spent the rest of the lesson avoiding Mr Morrison's questions and trying to work. When the bell went for the end of the lesson, she stuffed everything into her bag and followed Polly out of the classroom. They reached the door at the same time as Eve and Rhi. Lila stayed behind Polly, hoping to avoid Rhi's recognition.

"Shame about the earrings, Polly," Eve drawled, shouldering an expensive-looking leather rucksack. "Mind you, they were vile. No wonder they burned Mr Morrison's eyes out."

Lila was comforted to see Rhi look awkwardly at the floor. Clearly Eve's nasty streak didn't impress her best friend.

Eve shifted her attention. Lila felt her steely blue-grey gaze taking in her pristine uniform and neatly brushed hair, clearly assessing just how much of a threat she posed. Her eyes stopped on Lila's wrist where her blazer sleeve had ridden up. They widened maliciously. Too late, Lila realized her tattoo was on view.

"Nasty *graze* you have there, new girl," Eve commented. "It looks almost like a tattoo. But of course, tats are illegal if you're under eighteen. So it couldn't possibly be. Could it?"

"Leave her alone, Eve," Polly said. "Come on, Lila."

Lila's feet were rooted to the floor. Her good intentions of staying out of trouble were dangerously close to collapse. Polly hadn't deserved that crack about her earrings. She didn't deserve this treatment either. Because she dared to talk to Ollie? Who did Eve think she was, throwing her weight around like she owned the place? A bubble of anger starting rising in her blood. It boiled over, strong and fierce.

She met Eve's gaze head-on.

"Why don't you ask the guy who tattooed 'Ice Queen' on your arse?" she asked.

There was a shocked silence. Eve stared at Lila like she couldn't believe her ears.

"*What* did you say?"

OK, so Lil had just broken through, Lila thought. But it was worth it for the look on the Ice Queen's face.

"You heard me," she said. "Come on, Polly. It smells like a tin of old tuna around here."

THREE

"You shouldn't have said that," Polly muttered, hustling Lila away from the classroom.

"Eve Somerstown is a bully!" The Lil part of Lila was still fired up. "You have to stand up to bullies, or they trample you."

The look Polly gave her was a combination of awe and exasperation. "Eve's the most popular girl in the school. Her dad owns half of Heartside Bay. Making an enemy of Eve Somerstown is like . . . I don't know, getting through immigration and shooting the president."

"Some president!" said Lila.

Why wasn't Polly thanking her? She just got them

both out of trouble! A small voice in her head muttered something about frying pans and fires. She tried to ignore it.

"Just watch your back," advised Polly. "Eve's like an elephant subscribed to text alerts. She doesn't forget."

The way she said it sent a chill down Lila's back. Just like that, her anger boiled away, leaving Lila to face an unpleasant truth. Eve Somerstown sounded like the kind of girl who knew how to bear a grudge. Lila knew she had just made a huge mistake.

Her sudden anxiety must have shown in her face.

"Hey, don't listen to me," Polly added. "I get stressed about stuff like this, but it's clear you can stand up for yourself." She glanced at Lila's neatly buttoned collar. "You're kind of a surprise," she said thoughtfully. "You know that?"

Lila's phone vibrated.

Talk 2 me xx

Her fingers strayed to her tattoo. On top of everything else that had happened that morning, she really couldn't face Santiago. She wanted to forget about him. Didn't he realize that?

She'd hardly put her phone back in her pocket when it buzzed again.

TALK 2 ME LIL xxx

She tapped out a swift, irritable reply.

GO AWAY

Buzz. Buzz. Buzz. The texts all said the same.

Miss u. Love u xxx

"You should put that away before someone confiscates it," Polly told her. "They're really strict about phones here. Apparently there's a whole room in this place full of confiscated hardware."

Buzz. Buzz.

"I'm trying to," said Lila helplessly.

"Someone really wants to talk to you," Polly said.

"It's no one important."

Lila shoved her phone in her pocket. *Don't ask me anything else*, she thought imploringly. The thought of talking about Santiago, even to someone as sympathetic as Polly, made her blood run cold.

To her relief, Polly dropped the subject. "What's your next class?" she asked, peering at the paper in Lila's hand.

"History."

Polly pointed down the corridor. "History's that way. You OK finding it by yourself?"

Lila was jolted out of her thoughts. "You don't do history?"

"Don't panic, Eve doesn't either," Polly said kindly. "You'll be fine. Just don't call anyone else a tin of old tuna, OK? See you in maths."

Lila was surprised how nervous she felt, hearing Polly's shiny patent-leather brogues tapping out what sounded like a final farewell down the corridor. It was so hard, keeping everything together in this strange new place.

Buzz.

Going crazy without u xxx

Lila felt exhausted. When would Santiago get the message? She couldn't deal with him right now. As her thumb hit the *off* button, she ran into her second person of the day.

"Hey, watch where you're going!" said an irritated voice.

Lila almost dropped her phone. She looked up to apologize to whoever it was she'd trodden on. She recognized him from English that morning as the boy who had been staring at her: tall and geeky with short hair the colour of chestnuts. His heavy glasses had slid down his nose and there was a pained look in his electric green eyes.

"Don't feel you have to apologize or anything," he said sarcastically. "I have one spare foot."

The apology she had been framing died on her lips. He shook his head and pushed through the classroom door in front of her.

Lila wanted to scream at the unfairness of it. She took several deep breaths to calm herself. It was no good. Her anger, damped down a little since her spat with Eve, roared up again like a freshly fanned bonfire. He hadn't even given her a *chance* to apologize! Back in London, Lil ate guys like him for breakfast. She couldn't let a sorry specimen like that one get her down.

The history teacher, Ms Andrews, was a lot more welcoming than Mr Morrison. She beamed at Lila from beneath a blond fringe.

"You must be Lila? Welcome to the class. I'm afraid we're a little full, but there's a seat next to Josh over there."

She pointed at the empty chair. Lila's heart plummeted as she registered who her neighbour would be. The guy from the corridor. She couldn't believe the morning she was having.

Rubbing his chestnut-coloured head, Josh regarded her over the tops of his glasses as Lila slowly sat down. His green eyes were no friendlier than they had been outside the classroom. The name *Josh Taylor* was written at the top of his book.

"I guess you're Josh," Lila said, to break the silence.

"Looks that way," he said drily.

"Lila."

There was silence again.

"I was going to apologize, you know," Lila blurted. She knew she sounded petulant but she couldn't help it. "Only you didn't give me a chance."

Josh pushed his glasses up his nose. "Apologizing isn't the fashion around here. It's easier to assume the worst."

He bent his head over his book. Lila felt another rush of annoyance. Didn't he have any manners?

She tried to concentrate on what the teacher was saying about post-war superpower relations. It wasn't easy, particularly as she had the sense that Josh was staring at her every time she looked towards the front of the class. She wished she was sitting next to someone friendlier, who didn't take so many notes.

Sneaking a glance, she was surprised to see Josh wasn't taking notes after all. He was sketching, clearly not paying any attention.

"So, Josh," said Ms Andrews, after a complicated explanation on the causes of the Cold War. "Recap for us. How did the Berlin Blockade affect relations in Europe?"

Lila allowed herself a private grin. She was going to enjoy this.

Josh laid down his pencil. "The Soviets wanted control over the whole of Berlin, not just the eastern sector where they were based. They blocked all supply lines – rail, canal and road networks – into those parts of Berlin controlled by the Allies. The West responded by dropping supplies into the city by air, embarrassing the Soviets into lifting the blockade eleven months later. Battle lines were drawn. From that point, the Cold War was inevitable."

Lila shut her mouth, which had fallen open. Ms Andrews moved on to someone else, then wrote up a set of instructions on the whiteboard.

Josh glanced at Lila's face. "Just because I'm a guy, it doesn't mean I can't multitask," he said, taking up his pencil again.

"I didn't say anything," Lila protested.

"You were thinking it, though."

He was infuriating. Lila's eyes rested on his drawing. It looked like a girl's face in profile. Straight nose, wavy hair. A mole set just above a curving cheekbone. Her hand lifted to her face in surprise, feeling the mole on her own cheekbone.

"Is that—"

He slammed his book shut. "The instructions on the board say to do this part in pairs," he said. "You go first."

Great, thought Lila, reaching slowly for her pencil. Why would Josh want to draw her? He couldn't stand her.

They got on with their work. Josh looked surprised as she got more than her share of questions right, and she felt a little stab of triumph. *I'm not as stupid as you think, geek boy*, she thought.

"Do you draw in class a lot?" she asked at the end of the class, as they packed up their belongings.

Josh shrugged. "Depends on the class."

"Were you drawing me?"

Josh shoved his book deep inside his bag. "Are you always this nosy?"

Lila flushed. She was only expressing an interest. If he'd been drawing her, she had a right to know why. What was his problem?

"Are you always this rude?" she demanded.

"Am I rude?" He seemed surprised by the question.

Lila could hardly frame her answer, she felt so annoyed. "You're the rudest guy I've ever met!"

Josh finished packing his bag in silence. Lila could feel her whole body trembling with irritation as they walked out of the history classroom side by side. If they had maths together, she promised herself she would sit as far away from Josh Taylor as she could.

FOUR

As they turned into the corridor, Josh looked at her.

"Sorry," he said a little awkwardly. "I didn't mean to be rude."

So you're talking to me now? Lila thought, turning her phone on. She wasn't prepared to forgive him quite yet.

"Friends?" he said.

"Don't push it," Lila muttered.

"Acquaintances, then."

"I can do acquaintances," Lila conceded after a moment. She allowed herself to smile at him. When he smiled back, it transformed his face.

"So," he said. He sounded nervous. "As an acquaintance, can I ask you a question?"

"What?"

He scratched his ear. "Can I—"

Buzz.

They both looked at Lila's pocket. Josh looked annoyed by the interruption.

She pulled her phone out of her pocket.

CANT LIVE WITHOUT U CALL ME BABY PLEEEEEZ xxx

"They confiscate those," Josh said.

"Tell me something I don't know," Lila said irritably.

"Lila!"

Ollie was skidding down the corridor towards her. She was relieved to see a friendly face.

"How was history?" Ollie glanced at Josh. "Between them, Josh and Ms Andrews probably bored you to death. Give this guy a chance and he'll tell you everything about Hitler right down to the size of his socks."

"At least I can talk about something other than football," said Josh mildly.

Buzz. Buzz.

"They confiscate phones around here," said Ollie.

"I *know*," Lila sighed.

More kids joined them as they funnelled towards the maths block. With relief, Lila saw Polly's blue-black hair in the scrum, but the sight of Eve's red mane as well made her uneasy again.

Buzz. Santiago couldn't keep doing this. It wasn't fair.

Lila wasn't sure how it happened. One minute she was upright. The next, for the second time in as many hours, she was lying flat on her back among a sea of surprised faces with her belongings scattered everywhere.

When would her life stop being such a farce?

She suddenly glimpsed Eve's face in the crowd. It was triumphant. Now she thought about it, she had felt something trip her up. She glared at Eve, but didn't say anything. She wouldn't give her the satisfaction.

Ollie and Polly's faces loomed over her.

"Are you OK?" asked Polly in concern.

"I tripped over my shoelace," she said shortly.

"You have to stop falling at my feet like this," Ollie quipped. "People will talk."

She couldn't help but feel a little better looking into his smiling eyes. He helped her to pick up her books, which had scattered halfway down the corridor. Polly picked up the stuff which had rolled in the opposite direction. Lila looked around the gathered crowd, but Josh had vanished.

"Josh hates drama," Ollie said, noticing the way Lila was looking around. "You won't see him again today. No loss. 'At least I can talk about something other than football.' Right! Roll up for conversations on the most boring subjects in the universe!"

"It's OK, Ollie," said Polly, returning with several biros and Lila's calculator. "We all know you're threatened by Josh's intellect."

"Hey!" Ollie protested.

Polly shrugged her shoulders. "What can I say? The brain shop was all sold out when it was your turn."

Lila giggled at the look on Ollie's face. It felt really good to laugh again.

"It takes brains to play football too, you know,"

Ollie insisted. "But you don't hear me going around boring everyone about that, do you?"

Lila and Polly both raised their eyebrows.

"I seem to remember something earlier today, about a match where you thrashed the other side," said Lila. "Seven nil, wasn't it? 'Of course, it's a team game, but I scored most of the goals. . .'"

"OK, bad comparison," Ollie admitted. "But you know what I mean. Josh Taylor's a pompous idiot."

"And you're certainly not pompous, Ollie," said Polly innocently.

"Exactly," said Ollie, failing to pick up on Polly's sarcasm.

Polly grinned at Lila. Lila grinned back, sharing the joke. Suddenly she felt like maybe she could survive at Heartside after all.

Her phone had landed near Ollie's feet. He picked it up. Like it was happening in slow motion, Lila saw him take in all the texts from Santiago.

"Whoa," said Ollie. "These are, uh . . . pretty gushy."

Lila's face was burning up all over again. Ollie was going to think she had a permanently red complexion.

"My ex," she said, snatching the phone from his hand.

Ollie's expression was a mixture of surprise and curiosity. "How 'ex' are we talking?"

"Very."

Polly was looking interested now. "Same person who was texting you earlier?"

Lila prayed that Ollie and Polly would lose interest in this line of conversation, and fast. But there was no chance of that.

"The guy still sounds pretty keen," Ollie said.

"Was it someone in London?" Polly asked.

"Do you mind if we don't talk about this?" Lila begged. "I can't take much more drama today."

Ollie gave a slow smile. Lila had a flashback to the way he had looked when he pinned her against Mr Morrison's door at the start of her whole disastrous day. It already felt a lifetime ago.

"You're a mystery, Lila Murray," he said. "I like mysteries."

"As long as they aren't too complicated," Polly quipped. "See you in there, guys."

Lila spotted Rhi approaching Eve by the maths

classroom door as Ollie handed her the last stray book that had fallen from her bag.

"Time to get out of here," she muttered. She looped her arm quickly through Ollie's.

"Fine by me," he said, looking pleased.

As she towed him into the classroom, Lila risked a glance at Eve and Rhi. Eve's face was thunderous at the sight of Ollie and Lila arm in arm.

Suddenly, Rhi frowned at her in sudden recognition. Leaning towards Eve, Rhi whispered something in her best friend's ear. Lila swallowed. Now Rhi had figured out who Lila was, what kind of ammunition was she giving Eve to use against her? She had plenty, Lila knew that much. She wasn't proud of the way she had treated Rhi. She'd been a different person back then. But how could Rhi know that?

Leaving the past behind was going to be much harder than she'd thought. When would the shadow of Lil go away? And with the way she'd just flaunted Ollie in front of Eve, she hadn't exactly done herself any favours.

FIVE

As the bell finally went for the end of the day, Lila struggled to pack away her books, get out of her seat and leave the IT suite. She dragged her feet down the corridor, hoping she wouldn't bump into Eve or Rhi on her way out.

At lunch she had sat with Polly. Although she smiled at the kids she recognized from her morning classes, everyone scurried past the table without even acknowledging her. She guessed Eve had made her feelings clear to the entire year. She could practically hear the Ice Queen's drawling voice in her head, warning everyone off the new girl. Only halfway through day one, and she was already a pariah. Even Polly's company couldn't change that. She hadn't seen Ollie again all day.

Josh had sat a couple of tables away with an apple and a well-thumbed book. He didn't look in her direction once. Not even to ask if she was OK after her fall in the corridor.

Clearly he didn't actually want to be friends, she thought crossly. Ollie's description of Josh as a pompous idiot was right.

A pair of goggles had hidden Eve's steel-grey eyes for most of science that afternoon, but Lila had still felt her cold gaze boring through her shoulder blades. IT hadn't been much better. She now had a blinding headache and her new school shoes were rubbing her heels. And on top of everything else, she dreaded what she would find when she turned on her phone again after school. She couldn't wait to get out of here and hide in her bedroom for a while.

She gloomily spun the combination lock on her locker. Part of her was bracing herself for a box of eggs or something to come tumbling out. *Even someone as all-powerful as Eve Somerstown can't open locked doors,* she reminded herself. Still, she flinched as something fluttered out and drifted to her feet.

Bending down, she picked up the piece of paper and

smoothed it out. Someone had stuffed it through the vent on the front of her locker. She stared at the words.

Take heart. First impressions are misleading. You're a cool person with a clever head. Things will get better.

She studied the writing curiously, then turned the note over. There was no signature.

A funny warm feeling spread through her belly. Someone had bothered to write this for her. Someone knew how she was feeling. How was that possible?

She looked up and down the corridor. Other Year Tens were moving around the lockers, talking and joking. None of them were looking at her, or at the note in her hand.

She stared again at the writing. It was the nicest thing that had happened all day. In one swoop, she didn't feel alone any more.

"Ready to go?"

Polly was standing by her locker, clutching her bag to her chest. Lila saw that she'd put her zigzag earrings back on.

"Did you write this?" She waved the note. It seemed like something Polly might do.

"Nothing to do with me." Polly took the note from Lila's fingers and read it. "That's really cute!" she said with pleasure. "He's right, you know. Things will get better."

Lila snatched the note back. "How do you know it's a he?"

"I don't," said Polly gleefully. "But it's a safe guess. After the day you just had, it looks like you've got a secret admirer!"

Lila studied the note again. A secret admirer? Was this some sort of practical joke?

She gripped Polly's arm. "Swear to me that this isn't a wind-up."

"I swear!"

"Then it's some kind of weird Heartside Valentine's Day tradition," Lila said suspiciously. "You take Valentine's Day pretty seriously in this town."

"We do parades, not mystery notes. Stop looking so worried. It's exciting! Maybe it's a really hot guy who saw you in the canteen and couldn't bring himself to talk to you."

Lila felt a little thrill at the thought of this mystery guy.

Her mood was abruptly punctured by the sight of Eve heading towards the lockers, flanked by Rhi and two other girls.

"Let's get out of here before the queen bee ruins your buzz," said Polly. "Do you want a tour of your new town?"

Lila thought of her half-unpacked bedroom. Heartside Bay was her home now – it would be good to explore it a little. And with Polly for company, a tour could be nice.

"Sure," she said with a grateful smile.

They headed out into weak sunlight and a stiff breeze blowing in from the sea. Kids withdrew as Lila and Polly walked down the steps, and whispered together in groups. Lila's stomach clenched again.

"You would tell me if I smelled, wouldn't you?" she muttered.

Polly sighed. "Eve's word is law around here. Ignore them. I'll take you to the beach to take your mind off things. I often go to the sea when I'm feeling down. It's really soothing."

The walk to the beach took Lila's mind off her problems. The houses by the sea were all different sizes and shapes, with several old fisherman's cottages that had been turned into boutique bed and breakfasts and cute holiday cottages for couples who came to Heartside Bay to get married and enjoy themselves in Britain's most romantic town.

"The Old Town is cute," Polly said, noticing Lila's gaze, "but no one really lives here full time. It can flood during bad winter storms. You live up by the cliffs, right?"

"How did you know?" said Lila in surprise.

Polly shrugged. "Everyone lives up here. Let's take these steps. They go down to the beach."

Seaside towns in winter felt a little sad, Lila thought. Even tourist traps like Heartside Bay had a February melancholy about them. It matched her mood. Most of the ice-cream parlours and arcades along the front were closed for the winter. The pier was shuttered up as well. The Grand Hotel loomed over everything, its Regency walls and windows as pink and white as a frosted cupcake.

Lila's eyes were drawn to the fine white sand

stretching out into the grey sea, gently ruffled by the outgoing tide. Gulls wheeled overhead in the chilly air.

"Welcome to Bottom Bay," Polly joked.

Lila laughed. "You think it looks like a bum too? I felt bad for thinking that!"

"You have to be blind not to see the similarity," Polly grinned.

Lila noticed someone perched on a wall by the foot of the pier. Josh Taylor's chestnut-coloured head was bent over a sketchbook, his chin tucked into a scarf that he wore tightly wound round his neck to keep out the cold. He was alone.

"Doesn't that guy ever stop drawing?" she asked a little waspishly.

Polly followed Lila's gaze. "Josh Taylor is our local mystery. He's perfectly nice, and clever too, as you've probably figured out. But he's really private. No one knows much about him. He lives with his grandfather somewhere in the Old Town. He's always down here by himself, sketching."

Lila felt a reluctant glimmer of kinship with Josh Taylor. It sounded like he was as much of an outsider as she was.

"I thought you said no one lived in the Old Town," she said.

"That's typical of Josh. Doing stuff no one else does."

Lila remembered Ollie's remarks in the corridor earlier. "Ollie thinks he's pompous."

"Don't take anything Ollie says too seriously," said Polly. "Now I'm going to show you something to cheer you up."

She pointed out of the curving harbour, to a tiny island. Lila stared at it.

"What's so special about a lump of rock?" she asked curiously.

"That lump of rock is called Kissing Island. You can only walk to it when the tides are just right. It's Heartside legend that if you kiss your true love on Kissing Island at midnight of a full moon, you will be together for ever."

How romantic, Lila thought, jolted out of herself.

She had loved Santiago, or thought she had, but he had never felt like a *true* love – not like the kind that Polly was describing. She gazed at the little island with fresh eyes, and imagined a full moon, the light shining on the sea, and a gorgeous guy's lips coming in for the ultimate kiss. Ollie's, maybe. She put her hand into her pocket, feeling the mystery note lying snuggled up against the lining.

"Imagine," Polly sighed.

"I am," Lila sighed back.

A shaft of sunlight broke through the winter clouds overhead. The ray of light caught the white sand of the beach, making the grains sparkle and shine beneath Lila's feet, and the waves looked bright blue instead of grey. In that moment, Heartside Bay felt like the most beautiful, romantic place in the entire world, a place where anything could happen. Lila held her breath, not wanting to break the spell.

Then the sun went in again and everything returned to normal. Lila sighed and shivered a little inside her blazer. The wind coming off the sea was cold. Feeling in her pocket for her phone, she turned it on. Ten texts and two missed calls from Santiago. She couldn't face reading the texts.

"Do you want to come back to my house?" she asked, shoving her phone back into her pocket. "Hang out for a bit? When I say 'hang out', by the way, I basically mean 'help me unpack'."

Polly beamed. "I'd love to."

"We have to find it first," Lila warned jokingly. "I *think* it's that way."

They headed away from the beach and towards the cliff road. Polly chatted beside Lila as they walked, and the journey – which had felt like miles that morning – went by in a flash.

"This is it," said Lila, stopping outside the white gate of her house. "No one will be in yet – Mum and Dad are both still at work. But I have a key, and. . ."

Her voice trailed away.

The front door was wide open.

SIX

"I thought you said no one was in," said Polly, looking warily at the door.

"I did," said Lila. She moved slowly up the path.

"Come back!" Polly sounded frightened. "You don't know who might be in there!"

Lila's heart was pounding in her chest, but she kept moving. Different scenarios flew through her mind. Burglars, was her first thought. Most of their valuable possessions – TV, laptops – were still in handy carry-out boxes. Talk about a burglar's dream!

"You're not going in there alone," said Polly bravely behind her. "If we need it, I have the loudest scream in Heartside Bay."

Santiago, was Lila's second thought. Feeling a little

hysterical as she tiptoed on towards the door, she pictured Santiago's wild black hair and moody black eyes as he ran towards her, holding out his arms and demanding to know why she wasn't answering his texts or calls.

The tiled hall was still and quiet. Lila cocked her head and listened carefully for movement. Polly crept inside behind her.

Before they could react, two guys came thundering down the stairs towards them. Polly screamed and tugged Lila back towards the front door as the figures jumped on Lila and wrapped her up in a huge hug.

"All right?" said the taller one cheerfully.

"Loving the uniform," said the other, giving Lila a dig in the ribs.

"GET OFF HER!" Polly shrieked, still trying to heave at Lila's arm. "WE'LL CALL THE POLICE!"

"It's OK, Polly," Lila said breathlessly. "These are my brothers, Tim and Alex. You scared the life out of us! Why didn't you say you were coming down? Mum's not expecting you until the weekend!"

"We thought we'd surprise you," said Alex.

Lila pressed her hand to her heart and sank down on the bottom stair. "Well, you succeeded!"

"I just grew older by twenty years," Polly groaned.

"Cool," said Tim. "I like older women."

"Tim is rubbish with girls," Lila informed Polly. The shock was starting to wear off. "He thinks he has all these amazing lines that girls go mad for—"

"They do," Tim added, winking and smoothing his green hoodie down over his stomach.

"—when in fact they just think he's a massive idiot," Lila finished.

"Lil's right," said Alex as Tim started protesting. "When was your last date again? Was it last year, or the year before?"

"Ha ha," said Tim, pushing his older brother in the shoulder. He winked at Polly again. "So do you fancy a date, Lil's friend? As you can hear, I'm a bit out of practice."

"You could take her dancing at the Grand Hotel on the front," Alex grinned. "I hear the waltz is the latest thing."

He grabbed Tim around the waist and started dancing around the hall with him.

49

"Get off!" Tim shouted.

Polly was standing by the front door and looking like she wanted to bolt. Lila felt anxious. It would be typical if her brothers scared off the only friend she had in this place.

"It's Lila now, by the way," she said, waving to get Tim and Alex's attention. "Not Lil."

"You'll always be Lil to us," said Alex, dropping Tim.

"Ickle Lilzy-wilzy," Tim snorted.

"Just remember, OK?" Lila said. She dragged Polly up the stairs. Tim and Alex were still laughing behind them about the "Ickle Lilzy-wilzy" thing, but at least they didn't follow them up.

"Sorry." Lila showed Polly into her airy room with its cardboard boxes piled to the ceiling. "They're fools, but they're harmless. They won't be around much – Tim's at college in London and Alex is at uni."

Polly seemed different here to how she was at school, Lila realized. Quieter, and less confident.

"It was just a shock," Polly confessed. She hesitated. "Are they always like that?"

"Pretty much," Lila said.

They settled down to unpack Lila's boxes. Clothes, books, make-up, ornaments, magazines – everything came tumbling out. Before long the room was a tip, without a millimetre of carpet to be seen.

Polly put a magazine on top of a pile near the wardrobe, and straightened the edges so the magazines all lined up. "Why did you change your name?" she asked.

Halfway through packing her chest of drawers, Lila hesitated. She was still unsure how much of her past she wanted to share.

"I did . . . some bad stuff in London. I want to leave it behind, you know? Changing my name feels like a clean start."

Polly eyed the magazine stack again, and straightened it minutely. "The guy who texted you," she said. "Is he part of it?"

Lila nodded.

"With Eve's behaviour today, you probably wish you were still in London."

"Believe me, I don't," Lila said firmly.

Polly stopped playing with the magazine at the

sound of a car drawing up outside. She peeked through the curtains.

"It's the police!" she said, wide-eyed. "Someone must have heard me scream earlier and called them. What do we do?"

Lila saw a police officer getting out of the squad car parked by the kerb. Her tummy did its usual jumpy thing. *It's stupid to feel this nervous every time*, she thought a little hopelessly. She hadn't even done anything! But old habits died hard.

"What are we going to say?" Polly gabbled in panic. "It's a crime if you call the police for no reason!"

"Don't worry, it's just my dad," Lila said, dropping the curtain back into place. "He's a police officer." She decided not to explain that her dad was the new chief of police in Heartside. It was too embarrassing. "Come and say hi."

Polly straightened the edge of the curtain so it hung better. Her new friend was clearly a bit of a neat freak, Lila thought. No wonder Lila's house had spooked her.

Lila's dad looked sharply at Polly as the girls came downstairs.

"Dad, this is Polly," said Lila, waving her hand in introduction.

"Pleased to meet you," said Polly.

Lila's dad put his peaked cap on the hall table, and wiped a bit of dust off the brim. The braiding on his shoulders caught the light.

"The official title is Chief Murray," he said. Then he smiled. It reminded Lila of the flash of sunlight they'd seen on Heartside beach earlier. "But you can call me Greg."

Lila wanted to cringe. That was typical of her dad. Unnerving you one minute, and turning friendly the next. Polly smiled back uncertainly.

"How was your first day, Lil?" asked her dad. "Not in trouble yet, I hope."

Why did he have to embarrass her with a question like that? It wasn't much of a morale boost. She was trying her best. At some point he had to forgive her.

"I was a model student," she said shortly. "And I'm calling myself Lila now."

"Oh yes, your mum told me," said her dad in a jovial voice. "Talking of which, is your mum back yet? I'm starving."

The front door opened on cue. The smell of heavily vinegared fish and chips wafted down the hall, bringing Tim and Alex tumbling out of the living room and adding to the general squeeze at the foot of the stairs.

Lila's mum peered over a stack of greasy paper bags at the crowd in the hallway. "Boys!" she protested as Tim and Alex peppered her cheeks with kisses. "You should have let me know you were coming. I've only got fish and chips for three." She caught sight of Polly. "Oh, hello. . ."

"I'd better be going," said Polly, backing towards the front door.

Lila felt dismayed. Her family was a *nightmare*. "You don't have to," she said, starting after her friend.

"I do," Polly muttered, holding her bag tightly against her. "See you at school tomorrow, OK? Nice to meet you all."

She squeezed out of the front door and was gone.

"Polly!" Lila hurried through the front door. What had happened? Had she done something to annoy her? Had her dad? Her brothers? She felt panicky at the thought of school tomorrow, Polly ignoring her along with everyone else. But Polly had already vanished into the gloom.

"It's probably best, Lil," said her dad, in his bossy family-time voice as Lila came slowly back inside.

"It's *Lila* now, Greg," her mum scolded. She gave Lila an encouraging smile. "She seemed nice, love. Sorry I wasn't able to say a proper hello. Boys, get the plates out."

"First things first," said Lila's dad. He held out his hand. "Phones."

"I don't have to do that any more," said Alex. "I'm an *adult*, Dad."

"Yes you do," said Lila's dad firmly. "This is family time, whether you're fifteen or twenty. Hand it over."

Alex muttered, but passed over his phone. Tim did the same. They knew their dad too well to offer any serious argument. Lila was about to hand hers over too when she froze. She had remembered something crucial.

"Come on, Lila," said her dad impatiently. "There's a plate of fish and chips in the kitchen with my name on it."

She hadn't deleted the string of texts she'd got

from Santiago. The last thing she needed was her dad knowing she was still in touch with him.

"I . . . I think I left it in my room," she stuttered.

Buzz.

"I don't think so," said her dad, pointedly looking at her pocket.

There was a crash from the kitchen, and the sound of swearing. It sounded like her mum had dropped something. Her dad and her brothers all looked round at the interruption.

Seizing her chance, Lila yanked her phone from her pocket and frantically pressed DELETE ALL. The texts winked at her for a half a second, and the screen went blank.

She pressed her phone into her dad's outstretched hand. She hoped he couldn't feel the way her fingers were shaking.

That had been close.

SEVEN

Lila kept her head down on the walk to school the next day. The weather was colder and greyer than the day before, which didn't improve her mood. Who would ignore her today, she wondered glumly. Maybe Eve had moved things along with Ollie after school yesterday, at some really cool place where the kids of Heartside hung out together in the evenings and laughed about not inviting the new girl along.

By the time she reached the high street, she had created a whole world where Eve and Ollie were going out and her life here had become completely impossible. It was almost a surprise to see Ollie all by himself, waiting at the bottom of the steps. The collar on his blazer was turned up against the wind. It made him look even better-looking than usual. A couple of girls shot hopeful looks at him as they went past.

"About time you got here," he said, shivering.

Lila was surprised and grateful. "Were you waiting for me?"

"No, I just like hanging out on the steps in a gale," he joked.

He put his hands out and grabbed her. Lila almost stumbled backwards in surprise. He wasn't going to kiss her, was he? What would she do if he tried? There was no question that a kiss would cheer her up – and drive Eve mad with jealousy. It was almost worth doing just for that. But Lila Murray hadn't moved to Heartside Bay to kiss boys on her second day at school. Although maybe she could be persuaded. . .

Ollie squeezed her shoulders and then let go again. "Just checking you're still alive. I thought Eve might send a squad of assassins down your chimney in the night."

It was ridiculous to feel this disappointed. Did she seriously want her first kiss at Heartside to be on a set of concrete steps, in the wind and the cold, where everyone could see? It didn't exactly match the romance of a moonlit midnight on Kissing Island.

She forced a laugh. "They'd have trouble getting down the chimney. We don't have one."

The thought of going inside was more bearable with Ollie beside her. A reckless part of her wanted Eve to see them together, to prove that Eve's campaign against her wasn't working on the most important person of all. Was Ollie her secret admirer? She'd taken the note out last night and read it again. When she woke up this morning, it had still been clutched in her hand. Now it was folded up in her blazer pocket like a lucky talisman.

"What did you do last night?" Ollie asked as they climbed the steps together. "I would have hung around but I had football practice. The school pitches are right up on the cliffs. It was freezing."

Part of Lila wanted to punch the air in relief. Ollie hadn't been with Eve at all. She should have remembered the football practice thing; she'd even heard the PE teacher yelling at Ollie about it.

"Polly took me to the beach. We saw Josh."

Good move, Lila, she thought, feeling annoyed with

herself as soon as the words were out. *Mentioning another guy to the guy you're really interested in.*

"Don't tell me," said Ollie, rolling his eyes. "He was staring soulfully out to sea and drawing seagulls."

"I didn't see what he was drawing."

"He's not as interesting as he likes to think," Ollie said grumpily.

It dawned on Lila with a little thrill that Ollie was jealous. Maybe mentioning Josh hadn't been a bad move after all.

"Anyway," she said, trying to contain the smile she could feel growing on her face, "Polly came back to mine afterwards. I think my family freaked her out a bit."

"Why, have they all got two heads?"

Lila frowned. "She just went a bit funny and left. I hope she's OK. I could murder my family sometimes." She looked around. "Have you seen her this morning?"

"She'll be hiding somewhere, trying to stay out of Eve's way. There's nothing like invitation day to make a person feel welcome."

Lila frowned. "What's invitation day?"

"Forget it," said Ollie, suddenly looking awkward. "I have to go and have a word with Mr Slater – PE teacher, you met him yesterday. See you at break."

Lila watched him jog off down the corridor. Was it her imagination, or had Ollie just made that excuse so he wouldn't be seen with her inside school? And what was invitation day? Something else to worry about. She felt alone and exposed. Putting her hand in her pocket, she tried to draw strength from the feel of the note nestled into the lining.

She made her way towards the Year 10 corridor, looking for Polly's familiar hair in the crowd. She caught a drift of conversation from a group of girls she recognized from science the day before, and a flash of something sparkly in their hands.

"What are you wearing? Everyone takes the glamorous dress code really seriously, Eve won't let you—"

The girls stopped talking as Lila walked past. She hurried on towards her locker, aware of their eyes on her back. Why should she care what they were talking about? *I won't cry*, she thought fiercely.

She stopped dead. Eve was standing a little further

down the corridor, handing out sparkly envelopes and laughing with Rhi. She had put her hair up today, which made her neck look long and swanlike. She was beautiful, Lila thought wistfully. Beautiful and evil. For a brief moment she imagined what her life at Heartside would be like with Eve as her friend.

The relief she felt when she saw Polly waiting by her locker made her feel a bit dizzy. Only now could she admit how much she had been counting on Polly still being her friend. She wouldn't have been able to bear another day at Heartside High without her.

There was a red stripe in Polly's hair today, and red laces in her shiny brogues.

"Sorry about last night," Polly said as Lila approached. She looked embarrassed.

"Me too," said Lila fervently. "I was worried about you, but we hadn't swapped numbers yet so I couldn't call. I hope no one said anything horrible to you that made you leave? Tim and Alex can be—"

"It's no one's fault," Polly said. "My home life is a little different than yours. Quieter, you know? I was just a bit overwhelmed. That's all. Let's talk about something else."

Lila was happy to change the subject. There was something she really needed to know.

"Polly, what's invitation day?"

Polly nodded in Eve's direction. "The Ice Queen has a Valentine's party every year. They're incredibly glamorous. Each one is bigger and better than the last. There's always a band, and amazing decorations, and a love theme. Everyone talks about it for days beforehand, and weeks afterwards, about who kissed who and who wore what. I don't know what she's trying to prove. That Daddy has pots of money, I guess."

She sounded bitter.

"Don't tell me," said Lila. "You haven't been invited?"

"Of course not. I'm not in the cool gang any more. But you know what? I wouldn't go even if she had invited me. I've got more self-respect than that."

The way her hazel eyes flicked towards Eve handing out the sparkly envelopes told Lila a different story. Of course Polly wanted to go. Who wouldn't want to go to a party like that?

"That makes two of us," Lila said loyally. "Let's

make a date to hang out, OK? We can have a party of our own instead."

Polly laughed. "Sounds great. What band are you going to get?"

"Someone really big," Lila improvised. "Someone to wipe the floor with Eve's band."

Polly's eyes sparkled, getting into the game. "What's the theme?"

Before Lila could frame an answer, Ollie jogged around the corner.

"Slater wasn't there," he said a little breathlessly. "I'll catch him later. Want to head to class?"

Lila felt a rush of gratitude for Polly and Ollie. Maybe he didn't mind being seen with her. Whatever Eve Somerstown might do, at least these two were sticking by her.

There was a waft of lemony scent on the air. Polly's eyes darkened and Lila's heart gave an unpleasant thump. Eve had swished up to them. Lila didn't like the smile on her face one bit.

EIGHT

Ignoring Polly, Eve gave Lila a long calculating gaze. Then she switched her focus to Ollie.

"Hi, babe," she said sweetly, planting a slow kiss on Ollie's cheek. She wafted a sparkly envelope under his nose. "You are coming to my party, aren't you?"

"Am I?" said Ollie.

"Of course you are. Here's your invitation." She laughed, and ran her fingers through Ollie's sticking-up blond hair. "It's going to be a great night," she purred. "Even better than last year. I promise."

Ollie took the sparkly envelope with some caution, as if it were a bomb. Eve slid her perfectly manicured hand through the crook of Ollie's arm.

"Come on, or we'll be late for class."

Ollie looked thrown. "I was just waiting—"

"The new girl hasn't even got her locker open yet," Eve said, glancing at Lila. There was a look in her eyes that made Lila nervous. "The bell's about to go. Come *on*. . ."

"Nice to see you too, Eve," Polly said drily as Eve pulled a half-laughing, half-protesting Ollie away. "Come on, Lila, put your stuff away and let's go."

Trying not to feel downhearted, Lila fiddled with the latch on her locker. It felt strangely sticky. When she finally managed to get it open—

"Oh!"

She jumped backwards as a cascade of pink glitter and white confetti came pouring out. The glitter was the same colour as the sparkly invitations.

For a wild second, she felt a rush of hope. Maybe something from her secret admirer was hidden in the sparkles? She dug through the soft pink mess, feeling for an envelope, just in case. . .

"*Lila!*" Polly said in horror. "Look at you!"

Laughter rang out on all sides as Lila looked down at herself. Thick trails of pink glitter had run all the way down the front of her uniform. There were shiny little grains stuck to her skin, and her socks, and her tie. There was glitter in her pockets, and she could feel some trickling down inside her shoes. Glancing up, she caught sight of Eve smirking triumphantly as she towed Ollie towards their classroom.

She had been caught out by another of Eve Somerstown's dirty tricks.

Lila felt close to tears. She brushed at her blazer, but it was no good. The glitter stayed exactly where it was. She felt utterly stupid standing in the corridor covered in bright pink sparkles.

"Come on," Polly sighed. "I'll help you get cleaned up. We've still got a few minutes before the bell."

"It's no good," Lila groaned in despair. "Glitter's impossible to get rid of. I'm going to look like a piñata gone wrong all day."

Polly tapped her nose. "I've had all this and worse from Eve in the past. There's an extra uniform in my locker that you can borrow. Glitter-free."

Hope flickered in Lila's heart. "Are you serious?"

Polly shrugged. "It pays to be prepared. I learned that lesson a long time ago. My locker's open – help yourself. I'll explain everything to Mr Morrison so he won't mark you late, OK?"

"You're amazing," Lila breathed. Impulsively she gave Polly a hug.

Polly squirmed away, looking both pleased and embarrassed. "I don't fancy sharing your glitter, thanks," she joked.

"Sorry," said Lila, letting go quickly. "But you really are amazing."

Polly grinned. With sudden mischief in her eyes, she scooped a full handful of glitter from Lila's locker and ran after Eve's fast-disappearing back. A sudden cloud of pink sparkles filled the air, and Lila heard a scream of rage. Polly had dumped the glitter down the Ice Queen's back.

Feeling a little better, Lila pulled the spare uniform – blouse, tie and skirt – from Polly's locker and spun the combination lock shut behind her.

Holding the spare uniform away from her to avoid any glittery cross-contamination, Lila walked quickly to the toilet down the hall. She hung the uniform on the back of a cubicle door. She washed her hands and legs as best she could at the sinks, with the help of a handful of paper towels. Then she headed gratefully into her chosen cubicle and shut the door.

Leaning her head against the cool cubicle wall, she shut her eyes tightly and willed the tears away. Lila was stronger than this. She couldn't let Eve win.

She stripped down to her underwear, and wriggled into the fresh uniform. Polly's blouse fitted OK, and the tie of course was fine. She could live without a blazer for today. The skirt was a lot shorter than she would have liked – more along the lines of Lil than Lila – but it would have to do.

She turned her blazer inside out and wrapped her ruined uniform inside it. Then she tucked the bundle back under her arm and prepared to emerge.

Her fingers froze on the cubicle latch. Someone was coming into the toilets.

"I can't believe Polly Nelson thought that was funny," Eve raged. There was a *whoosh* from the sink taps. "She's such a bitch. I don't know why I was ever friends with her. I have glitter all down the back of my blouse."

"You started it, you know," said Rhi in her distinctive London voice.

"Lila Murray deserves everything she gets, the silly cow. You of all people should know that."

Lila flinched miserably inside her cubicle. Rhi had definitely told Eve about what had happened in London. She shouldn't have been surprised.

"Who does she think she is, coming here and smarming up to Ollie? He's mine. Everyone knows it. He doesn't fancy her, whatever people think. I bet she's gone running to Reception. 'Ooh, miss, they're all being horrible to me.' She's pathetic."

Lila's hand was still hovering on the cubicle latch. She hardly dared to breathe.

Eve was still ranting.

"Miss Goody Two Shoes is nothing special. Everyone will realize that soon enough. If she thinks she can come to Heartside and act all high and mighty, she's in for a nasty shock."

"Leave it, Eve," advised Rhi. "You haven't invited her to your party, and—"

"I'd rather invite a dead weasel," Eve said with venom.

Rhi continued as if Eve hadn't interrupted. "—and you've made it clear that you don't want anyone making friends with her. She's history around here already. There's no point starting a vendetta for the sake of it."

There was the scrunching sound of paper towels, and the flip of a bin lid.

"I love vendettas," Eve purred. "They're so much fun. Believe me, Rhi, that girl will rue the day she ever came to Heartside. The fun and games for Lila Murray are only just beginning."

NINE

Explaining why she was wearing someone else's uniform while her own looked like it had been caught in some kind of fairy explosion had been difficult. Lila had invented an art class and a box of glitter with a loose lid, and had just about got away with it.

"Typical," her dad sighed.

Lila bit her lip. As usual, her mum intervened.

"That's not fair, Greg. At least it wasn't a bottle of indelible ink. We have plenty of packing tape left over from the move. Wrap it round your hands, sticky side up, and rub it over your uniform, love. The glitter should come off without too much difficulty. Lucky that your friend had a spare one for you to borrow."

Lila had got through two rolls of packing tape that

evening, meticulously cleaning her uniform from top to toe until close to midnight. Despite her best efforts, she was still picking glitter out of her shoes, books and locker on Wednesday afternoon. Eve knew exactly how to cause maximum trouble with minimum effort.

The silent treatment from the other kids continued. Even Ollie seemed to have disappeared, sucked into the heart of Eve's gang and guarded jealously. Josh was his usual monosyllabic self, although he did smile at her these days. At least he didn't completely ignore her like everyone else. And all the time, Lila was wondering when Eve would strike again.

The conversation she had overheard in the toilets was burned into her memory. She cringed again and again as she imagined what Rhi had told Eve. In addition to keeping out of Eve's way, she now found herself swerving round corners and loitering behind doors whenever she saw her former friend as well.

By the end of school on Wednesday, total exhaustion was starting to set in. To help her cope with everything, Lila started making lists in her head of all the good things about Heartside. Polly. Ollie – when she saw him. The beach. Josh, at least when he smiled at her. Her new house, which was light and airy, with a garden and wide sea views; her old view in London had been of a row of dustbins, enlivened by the occasional urban fox. And best of all: no curfew, or mandatory meal times, or checking in with her parents at all hours of the day and night. Unlike in London, where she had been made to feel like a prisoner in her own life, her parents were giving her freedom in Heartside. She was free, and she wasn't going to mess it up again. All she had to do was fix the rest of the mess she was in, and her life would be great.

She had got much warier about opening her locker since the glitter incident. Prising it open cautiously at the end of Wednesday, she reached her hand in for her bag. As she did so, she managed to knock over a stack of textbooks. Her heart skipped as a note covered in familiar writing came fluttering out from between the pages of one of the books.

She snatched it up. Her heart was racing at a ridiculous speed. What would it say this time?

Not everyone at Heartside takes orders from Eve Somerstown. Do you know about karma?

Eve will get what she deserves, and so will you.
Have faith.

Once again there was no signature. The words weren't romantic, but they were just what she needed. Someone was looking out for her, and believing that things would get better. She checked quickly to make sure no one was looking. Then she pressed her lips to the note.

"Thank you," she whispered. "Whoever you are."

"Hey," said Polly, coming up behind her. "Let's get out of here. You need a pick-me-up, and I know exactly where we should go."

Lila quickly slid the little piece of paper into her pocket. It felt too precious to share, even with Polly. "Where's that?"

"The Heartbeat Café in the Old Town. It used to be a pub, but it was turned into a gorgeous coffee house years ago. They do live music. All the local kids hang out there."

Lila raised her eyebrows. "Including Eve?"

"You can't avoid her in this town," Polly said with an apologetic shrug. "It's a great place, Lila. I'll show you the sneaky way in if you're worried about bumping into Eve. So, are you coming?"

Drawing strength from the new note in her pocket, Lila took a deep breath. "This is my town now, whether Eve likes it or not. The Heartbeat Café sounds perfect. Let's go."

The sun was nowhere to be seen as they walked from the school into the Old Town. Gulls sat on the uneven rooftops, crying and flapping their wings. To Lila it felt as if they were repeating what her secret admirer said. Have faith! Have faith!

The roads in the Old Town were narrow and higgledy piggledy, sloping left and right, some with steps and some with cobbles. Lila was lost in moments. She wasn't surprised tourists avoided this maze when they could spend their time on the wide, straight high street and the gently curving Marine Parade with its views of the sea instead.

Polly dragged her down a narrow set of cobbled steps to a silvery wooden fence, and pushed hard at the creaking gate. Inside there was a little paved garden dotted with wooden tables and large, furled umbrellas.

"That leads to the rooftop garden," Polly said, pointing at a spiral of rusty iron steps running up the side of the old white-brick building. "It's gorgeous in the spring, if you can face the climb. We're going in this way. This fire door's never locked."

They met a set of worn, carpeted steps as they entered the building. Polly ran up and craned her neck around the corner at the top. "Good, the table's not taken," she said, sounding relieved. "Come on."

"Oh!" Lila exclaimed when she reached the top. "It's so cool!"

The Heartbeat Café hummed like a hive below them, full of clatter and chatter. The red leather booths that lined the panelled walls were already half full, particularly the booths near the stage. Lila spotted Eve at once, sitting with her back to the balcony, beside Rhi and opposite a boy with dark curly hair she didn't recognize. She nudged Polly.

"Who's that?"

"Max Holmes," Polly said promptly. "Tech genius with a rebellious streak. He's been going out with Rhi for about a year. Cute, isn't he?"

Lila caught a flash of Max's white teeth as he threw

his dark head back and laughed at something Rhi had said. "Very," she agreed.

"Eve always gets that booth by the stage," Polly said, settling down at the little balcony table. "People say it's the best spot, but I think it's better up here. You can see everything that's going on."

Lila noticed that there were hundreds of carved initals inscribed into the wooden walls around her. There were messages scratched into the wooden balcony rail too, and the banister that curved down the stairs. She traced the flowing letters *LW&TG* on a panel by her head.

"Carving initials and messages is a Heartbeat Café tradition," Polly smiled. "Heartsiders have been doing it for generations. We are the love capital of the world, remember."

Lila felt the love of *LW&TG* tingling through her as she traced their time-worn initials with her fingers. She wondered who they were and what their story had been. She wanted a timeless love like that. Maybe she'd find one at Heartside Bay. *Maybe I've already found it*, she thought, picturing the note in her pocket. *Only I don't know who with.*

Down below, Max Holmes was carving something into the wall beside the booth he, Rhi and Eve were sitting at. It wasn't hard to work out that he was adding his and Rhi's initials to the history on the Heartbeat Café walls. Rhi and Max seemed like the perfect couple as they smiled into each other's eyes and linked hands over the table, and Eve was laughing and teasing them both. They all looked very happy.

"I'll get us something to drink," Polly offered.

As she headed down the stairs for the bar, Lila looked back at Eve's booth. She blinked in surprise. An extra person had slid into the booth opposite Eve. His face was turned towards the balcony, and his eyes were on Lila.

Ollie slowly lifted his hand, apparently to scratch his ear. He quickly pointed upwards. Then he opened his hand, showing five fingers.

Lila guessed he meant the roof garden in five minutes. She could see Polly queuing at the bar. A reckless feeling swept through her.

Why not? she thought.

TEN

The rusty spiral steps up to the roof garden looked a lot more dangerous now that Lila was thinking of climbing them. Shivering a little in the cold, she set her foot on the bottom step and started to climb. The steps squealed and groaned as she passed. She held on to the handrail as tightly as she could.

And then suddenly the handrail wasn't there. It had rusted away to nothing, leaving a big drop to the concrete below. Lila felt sick. If she fell, she would break her neck! Focusing on thoughts of Ollie's bright blue eyes and mischievous smile waiting for her, she forced herself onwards, keeping as far away from the yawning gap as she could.

She caught her breath at the top, willed her

legs to stop shaking – and felt a punch of horrible disappointment.

The garden was halfway through a makeover, dotted with bags of compost, old pots, chicken wire and garden tools. There was a beautiful view: the town's old roofs spread out like a patchwork blanket below her, and Lila could see the sweeping bay with its bracketing cliffs. But Ollie wasn't there.

The wind from the sea blew her hair around her face. She could feel it getting tangled and curly. What was going on? Was this one of Eve's tricks? Suddenly she didn't feel safe up here. The wind was strong, and the walls around the edges of the garden weren't very high. Eve would love it if she fell off the roof.

There was no way she was going back down those rusty outside steps. Lila tried the handle on the rooftop door, which opened on to a dark, twisting staircase. She was shaken as she held on to the banister and made her way down.

She could hear voices now, drifting up from the café below her feet. She paused for breath on a tiny patch of landing beside a door, which suddenly flew open.

"Sorry," said Ollie as Lila staggered backwards,

almost tumbling down the second twisting flight of stairs. "I didn't see— *Lila!* Where were you?"

"Where were *you*?" Lila accused, trying to straighten her skirt and flatten her windblown hair.

"Waiting for you. I didn't see you come up the stairs."

"I thought you meant the roof garden." Her cheeks were heating up as usual. "I went up the fire escape."

Ollie's eyebrows shot up. "You're mad. That thing's a death trap!"

"I know that *now*," Lila said.

Several people were coming up the stairs. In the squash and squeeze of the narrow landing, Lila was pushed right into Ollie. She froze as his hands came around her back.

"I like your hair mussed up like that," he said, looking down at her with those deep blue eyes. "It suits you."

Their faces were so close. His mouth was inches away from hers. He was about to kiss her, she was sure of it. And she knew that she would kiss him back. . .

You hardly know him! she told herself desperately.

Her thoughts were in chaos. *Don't make the same mistakes you made in London!* But she didn't seem able to stop herself. Something was drawing her towards him.

He seized her hand. It felt warm in hers. "Listen," he said. "I really want to tell you something. Can we find a quiet place to talk?"

"About what?"

He dragged her all the way downstairs, away from the bar area and into a corridor ending at a disabled toilet.

"Perfect," he said in relief. He pushed open the door, ushering Lila inside, then locked it behind them.

Lila looked round the dingy little room with its buzzing overhead light. What was going on? Why were they hiding in here?

"I've known Eve a long time," Ollie began. "We were at primary school together. We don't live far apart, our parents are friends, and I know she wants to go out with me. The trouble is, I don't like her. Not in that way." His eyes softened. "But I do like you. I really like you. Eve just makes it impossible for me to go out with anyone else. I need to straighten things out with her before taking things any further, OK? I don't want anyone getting hurt. Can you be patient? Can you trust me?"

He ran his hands through his hair and gazed beseechingly at her. Lila felt a hopeless tug in her gut. She couldn't help herself. Even in a smelly toilet she felt herself falling for him. His gaze was smouldering. She leaned towards him. . . There was a hammering at the door. Lila and Ollie sprang apart.

"I know you're in there," Eve said furiously, hammering again. "Open the door!"

ELEVEN

Lila felt the blood draining from her face. Of all the people. . . How could she possibly explain that they had only been talking? OK, so they had nearly kissed. But it wouldn't look that way. It wouldn't look that way when she opened the door and faced the one person she really, really didn't want to see.

"I said, open it!" Eve shouted, banging on the door again.

Ollie looked as worried as Lila felt. "This is going to be nasty," he said. "But we can handle it. Right?"

You've had worse than this! Lil whispered in Lila's head. *Face her and get it over with! Unlike in the past, you have nothing to be ashamed of.* "I can if you can," she said shakily. An even nastier thought struck her. "Are you going to tell her what you just told me?"

Ollie looked uncomfortable. "It's not really a good time, is it?"

"There's never a good time for things like this." Wisdom was coming from somewhere and pulling Lila's scattered thoughts together.

He stared at her. "So I should do it now?"

"No!" Lila said quickly. She cringed at the thought of witnessing the conversation. "Don't do it where I can see it. OK?"

"Open the door," Eve bawled.

"Promise me," Lila begged.

There was more banging. Ollie flinched and rubbed his hands through his hair. "We'd better open the door before Eve kicks it in."

Lila reached out her hand and slowly turned the lock.

The door crashed open at once. A crowd of people were standing outside in the corridor. Eve's arms were tightly folded across her body, her face burning with anger. Rhi looked uncomfortable. Max was openly laughing. In the background, Lila couldn't make out Polly's expression at all.

"Eve," Ollie began, raising his hands. "This isn't what it looks like. I swear we weren't doing what you think we were doing."

"Don't lie to me," Eve spat. The look she gave Lila was incendiary. "Who locks themselves in a toilet just to *talk*? How long has this been going on?"

"Nothing happened!" Ollie repeated.

"I don't believe you," Eve raged.

Ollie's shoulders slumped. "OK, it's like this. Lila and I—"

Lila felt panicky. He was going to do it right here and now, she realized, with a swoop in her stomach.

She didn't like Eve, but being rejected by a boy in front of your friends? She wouldn't wish that on anyone. Despite herself, Lila felt a little rush of pleasure mixed in with the horror. Ollie *liked* her. Her heart fluttered just thinking about it. But rejecting Eve like this, out in public for everyone to see. . . Something told her that the Heartbeat Café grapevine would love it. The word was probably already spreading about her and Ollie being locked in the toilet together. A public humiliation like this would be one more reason for Eve Somerstown to hate her.

"Ollie," she began in warning.

Suddenly, the air split open. Rhi screamed and covered her ears as the fire alarm by her head started shrilling at full volume. A cry went up from somewhere.

"Fire!"

Doors burst open on all sides. Empty moments before, the corridor was suddenly full of running people. The cry passed among them, loud and fearful.

"Fire! There's a fire!"

The alarm wailed on like a banshee. Frozen to the spot, Lila thought of the old building they stood in: the old timbers, and the dry, threadbare carpets, the wooden stairs and the plush curtains that hung on either side of the stage. It didn't take much imagination to picture the whole place burning to the ground.

Ollie abandoned whatever he had been going to say. "We have to get out of here," he said urgently. "Where's the closest exit?"

Lila felt someone grab her arm. As she was pulled down the corridor, pushed and shoved on all sides by people trying to reach the exit, she noticed the fire alarm on the wall beside the disabled toilet door.

The handle pointed downwards. Someone had pulled it. But . . . that didn't make sense! There was no fire *here*.

"No need to panic! Everyone this way!" said a boy Lila recognized from behind the café counter. He stood calmly by the door into the bar, ushering frightened people past. "Exit through the kitchen."

Then it hit her. Eve had pulled the alarm to save face. She wasn't stupid. She knew Ollie had been about to dump her in public. She had created the perfect diversion.

Lila wanted to tell someone what Eve had done. But no one was looking at her or listening to her as she tried to speak. The alarm screamed on above her head, making it hard to think straight as she was pushed and jostled onwards.

The hand was still firmly on her arm. As she stumbled into the kitchens on a wave of people, she looked down – and recognized the silver watch on the wrist that held her.

Eve shoved her sideways, vicious and determined. Lila stumbled and almost fell through a half-open door to the left of the exit.

Eve's grey eyes drilled into her. Lila realized with a kick of adrenaline that this was the first time she and Eve had been alone.

"Let me put this really simply, new girl, so that even a lowlife like you can understand." Eve advanced towards Lila. "Leave. Ollie. Alone."

"We were just talking," Lila gasped, steadying herself against a nearby shelf. They were in a walk-in pantry, among shelves stacked with huge tubs of mayonnaise and ketchup. "There's no law against talking."

Eve curled her lip into a sneer. "Oh dear. Still not listening, are you? You think it's been bad so far? You have no idea what I can do to you. I can make your life hell. You can't waltz into Heartside and help yourself to my cookie jar."

"Ollie's not a cookie," Lila snapped, finding the courage from somewhere. "I know you pulled the fire alarm, Eve. You could get into a lot of trouble for that. I could tell someone."

Eve flicked the threat away like a fly. "Maybe it worked like that back in London, but it's not going to work here. I know about you, you see. I know you're a nasty piece of work. Rhi's little stories were very . . . illuminating on the subject of your past."

Lila squirmed helplessly. "Eve, you—"

"If you don't leave him alone, I will tell Ollie everything." Eve gave a giggle, relishing her power. "Every nasty little detail. When everyone hears what you're really like, you won't last five minutes in Heartside. But of course, they'll have to find you first. Won't they?"

With a smile and a little wave, Eve backed out of the pantry, shut the door – and locked Lila inside.

TWELVE

Lila ran to the door and pounded on it. A quick scan of it told her the bad news. No handle.

"Let me out!" she hollered. "Let me out of here!"

Eve wasn't there. No one was listening. Lila's heart jumped frantically in her chest. She pressed her ear to the door and listened, doing her best to keep calm. Feet were rushing past, trying to get outside. They hadn't realized there was no fire. No one knew Eve had set off the alarm, or that Lila was locked in here.

"Please!" she yelled.

No one came.

Soon even the muffled sound of running feet faded to nothing. Defeated, Lila sank on to the floor with her head in her hands. The room was small and dark, and the floor tiles were cold beneath her. Until someone opened the door from the outside, there was no escape. She shivered, and pulled her blazer more tightly around herself. It was cold in here, and likely to get colder. Outside it was getting dark. What if no one came back for hours? She could freeze to death.

Overwhelmed by everything, Lila felt the tears squeezing from the corners of her eyes. She didn't want to cry but she couldn't help it. She didn't deserve any of this. She was so tired of everything. Never before had the thought of London felt so appealing. She leaned her face into her knees and closed her eyes.

When she felt uncomfortably numb and cold, she got to her feet again. If she spread out her hands, she could almost touch the walls of her prison. The frosted glass in the tiny window looked thick and unbreakable. Fear gripped her round the throat. Food kept better in airtight conditions. How long before the oxygen ran out?

Stop terrifying yourself, Lila commanded. *Do something!*

She walked back to the door, folded her fingers into

a fist and started pounding again. Someone was bound to come eventually. Weren't they?

"Let me out! *Let me out!*"

She shouted until her throat felt raw, and hammered until her hands felt bruised.

Finally, the door opened.

"Lila?"

Lila gaped at her dad, standing there in his full police uniform. She felt a strange mixture of relief and apprehension.

"What are you doing here, Dad?"

Her father sighed. "I was going to ask you the same question! We've been looking for you everywhere. What happened?"

A hundred accusations jumped through Lila's head, quicker than lightning. The urge to get Eve Somerstown into trouble was overwhelming. But why would he believe her?

"Why were you hiding in here?" her dad asked with a frown.

He thought she'd been *hiding*? Lila wanted to groan. He didn't trust her any more than he had in London.

"I was . . . locked in," she managed.

"But what were you doing in here in the first place?" Still frowning, he looked around at the tins of beans, the huge plastic bottles of mustard and barbecue sauce. He snapped his gaze back towards at her. "I hope you weren't up to anything."

"I got locked in," Lila repeated numbly. She couldn't say it was Eve. Her father would only lecture her about blaming other people for your own mistakes. She'd heard that lecture a hundred times. And even if, by some miracle, he did believe her, Eve would make her life in Heartside Bay even more difficult than it already was. It wasn't worth it.

Her father fixed her with a hard stare. "Do you know who set off the fire alarm?"

"The person who found the fire, I guess," Lila said.

She hated herself for lying. Her first lie in Heartside Bay. So much for a new start.

"It was a false alarm," her father said, watching her closely. "Someone tripped it on purpose."

"Oh?"

Her father waited for her to say something else.

Lila kept her mouth shut. He sighed, a familiar mix of disappointment and disbelief.

"Come on, then," he said impatiently. He held open the pantry door. "Your friends have been worrying about you."

Lila followed him slowly out of the kitchen, towards the open back door. She was almost knocked over by Eve, who came racing towards her.

"Lila!" Eve's eyes were wide and anxious. "Are you OK? We've all been going crazy with worry! One minute you were with us as we left the building – and the next minute we couldn't see you anywhere! You scared the life out of us!"

Lila's whole body went rigid as Eve pulled her into a tight hug. Whatever she had been expecting, it wasn't this! Over Eve's shoulder she could see the others gathered in the Heartbeat Café's back garden: Rhi and Max, Ollie and Polly. They were all looking as surprised as Lila.

"How are you?" Eve insisted, as if she hugged Lila every day.

"Aren't you going to answer your friend?" said her father.

"I'm . . . fine," Lila said at last.

Being hugged by Eve felt like being choked by a poisonous jungle vine. After several seconds, Eve gave the appearance of reluctantly letting go.

"However can we thank you for finding her, Officer?" Eve said, looking up through her long eyelashes at Lila's dad.

"It's Chief Murray," he said. "I'm Lila's father."

Polly was the only one of the group whose face wasn't a picture of shock. It would have been funny if it hadn't been so embarrassing. Now she wasn't just the new girl trying to steal Ollie, but the daughter of Heartside's new police chief as well. *Can you be a double pariah?* Lila wondered in despair.

"Wow," said Eve, recovering first. "I'm very pleased to meet you, Chief Murray. I'm Eve, Eve Somerstown. My father has already told me a lot about you. I had no idea you were Lila's father!"

Lila was pleased to see that Eve's charm offensive totally failed. Her dad simply nodded, patted his pocket and pulled out a notebook.

"Can any of you tell me what happened in here this afternoon?" he asked, looking round at everyone.

"There was a fire," said Eve. She looked sweetly confused. "Wasn't there?"

"Someone pulled the alarm under false pretences. It has caused a great deal of confusion, and has lost the Heartside Café valuable business. They are understandably angry, and would like to discover the culprit."

Was she imagining it, Lila wondered unhappily, or did her dad shoot her a particular glance when he said that?

"None of us would do something like that on purpose," said Rhi.

The others looked just as shocked at the suggestion that someone had set the alarm off for fun. Lila had a feeling she was the only one who knew the truth.

"Lila?" her father rapped. "Have you remembered anything useful yet?"

Lila knew she should tell him the truth. Her dad hadn't risen through the ranks of the police for nothing. He could spot a lie a mile off.

"No," she said. "Nothing."

Her father raised his eyebrows. "You don't

remember who locked the pantry door on you either, I suppose?"

Lila could feel Eve's gaze boring into her. She shook her head. Perhaps her silence would make Eve like her a bit more. She hated herself for wanting Eve to like her.

With a sigh, her father put his notebook away. "Time to go home, everyone. Lila, I'll give you a lift."

Eve towed Ollie away. Rhi did the same with Max. Lingering briefly, Polly gave Lila a look that was part sympathy, part something else. Before Lila could put her finger on it, her father had taken her firmly by the arm.

"The car's out the front."

Lila had barely settled herself in the front seat of her dad's squad car before it began.

"I don't like the crowd you've got involved with, Lila," her father began, turning the car around and heading out of the town centre. "How can you expect me to trust you when something like this happens and you lie to me?"

Lila wanted to say she hadn't lied. But she had. So she stayed quiet.

"Heartside Bay is supposed to be a fresh start," her father continued.

Lila closed her eyes. She knew what was coming next.

"I think," said her father seriously, "you need to spend some time thinking about why we moved here in the first place. We cannot have that happen again."

THIRTEEN

Lila kept to herself for the next couple of days. It wasn't hard, because Polly, Ollie and, weirdly, Josh were the only people who spoke to her. Polly was acting like the whole thing at the Heartbeat Café had never happened, while Ollie gave her lots of flirty smiles, which Lila appreciated. Josh said hi when they saw each other in class, but still not much else. The rest of the school continued to ignore her in the classroom, corridor and canteen like she had a contagious disease. She heard a few whispers on Thursday afternoon about her dad being the new chief of police as she walked around with her head bowed over her books. The gossip hadn't taken long to get around.

After the Heartside Café disaster, her dad had told

her to come straight home after school for the rest of the week. The weather was vile on Thursday, so she had been glad to trudge up the hill back to her cosy room. Now that everything was unpacked, it was starting to feel more like home. Lila sorted out her bookshelves and clothes cupboards, throwing out old Lil-style outfits and trying not to dream of Ollie. But Friday dawned bright and clear, and by lunchtime she was feeling stir crazy and craving a walk to the beach.

It hadn't taken long for the seaside to take hold of Lila's heart. There was something about the wide horizon, the scudding waves, the gulls and the smell of salt and the sense of a huge world beyond the sea that made her feel better than anywhere else in Heartside. She took herself down to the beach as soon as she finished lunch. Polly would probably have come with her, she thought, but today she wanted to be alone.

She stood with her feet in the sand and her hands deep in her pockets, the wind tugging at her hair and cheeks. There was a ship on the horizon, sending plumes of smoke from its stacks into the blue sky. Lila wished she was on it, and sailing far away from here, somewhere where the ocean and the clouds above were all she could see.

Josh was sitting in his usual place by the pier, drawing in his sketchbook. An apple sat beside him. As if he felt her looking, he glanced up. Their eyes met.

Lila wasn't sure what to do. Should she call out? Go over and speak to him? She settled for lifting her hand awkwardly and waving. His pencil looked like a conductor's baton as he waved it back.

Her phone started buzzing. Still wondering about Josh, Lila answered it without thinking.

The voice on the other end was deep, with a hint of an accent.

"I thought you were *never* going to answer your phone, Lil."

Blood rushed into Lila's cheeks. "Santiago?"

"Of course it's me. It's so good to hear your voice. How are you?"

What was she doing? *Hang up!* she told herself urgently. But her fingers wouldn't obey.

"I'm broken-hearted, baby," he whispered. "I miss you so much, I am thinking of tattooing your initials on my left arm, to match the right. I need to talk to you."

She glanced at her own tattoo. It had seemed like such a romantic thing to do – to get each other's initials etched on to their wrists. She'd been such an idiot. Now, even though the tattooist had reworked the initials so they looked like an abstract pattern, she could still see the SG threaded through the centre of the swirling heart. He was, quite literally, in her blood.

"Talking's not a crime, you know," he said temptingly.

His words reminded Lila of what she'd said to Eve in the Heartbeat Café. Talking to a guy wasn't the same as seeing him, was it? She and Ollie were proof of that. In the midst of the mess that surrounded her in this strange new place, all Lila wanted was to feel normal. It would be so nice, just talking to someone who liked her. Someone she didn't have to explain things to, or hide who she really was from.

"Fine," she said, feeling a strange mixture of relief and guilt. "Let's talk."

"I can't stop thinking about you," he said at once. "When can I see you?"

Whoa! she thought, feeling alarmed. This was already getting out of hand. She should have hung up when she had the chance.

"It's difficult," she said helplessly. "I'm here, you're in London. It's over."

His voice caressed her. "Heartside is not so far away. I can come and visit. I like the sea."

"No," Lila said quickly. "That would be a really bad idea. My parents would kill me if they knew I was talking to you—"

"Why do they need to know?"

She closed her eyes and pinched the bridge of her nose. "This is a fresh start for me, Santiago. Don't you understand? No more lies."

"There's a difference between lying and not saying anything at all, Lil. Meet me. Please?"

A memory of Santiago's dark, laughing eyes and thick ebony-coloured hair made Lila's heart thud. They had spent some great times together. He was exciting and a little dangerous and for a while it had seemed so refreshing that he didn't just follow the rules like everyone else. Maybe she could meet him. . .

You're Lila now, not Lil! she told herself with some desperation. She had to be strong.

"No," she said. She felt calm again suddenly, knowing she'd made the right decision. "Please don't call or text me again, Santiago. You know I can't see you."

With the last threads of her resolve, she hung up. Then she turned the phone off completely and stuffed it deep into her pocket. It pushed against the notes from her locker, making them crinkle.

She focused on her surroundings again, feeling dazed by the aching feeling in her heart. Realizing Josh wasn't sitting by the pier any more, she checked her watch – and gasped. Class started in ten minutes. If she didn't hurry, she would be late!

This is your fault, Santiago! she thought angrily, running as fast as she could to the steps leading up from the beach to the road. He was still making trouble for her, even from a distance.

Lila made it back into the reception area as the first bell went. She sped down the corridor, relieved that no one else was around, and threw herself through the door of her classroom just in time.

"Cutting it a bit fine, aren't you?" said Polly as Lila collapsed, panting, in her chair.

Lila paused. She still wasn't sure how Polly felt about the way she had vanished with Ollie on Wednesday.

Polly grinned, and Lila felt her shoulders drop in relief. Maybe they were OK after all.

She was about to open her bag and pull out her books when one of the school secretaries put her head around the door.

"Can Lila Murray go to the office, please?"

There were a few mutters, and a couple of glances in Lila's direction. Eve smiled sweetly and drew her finger across her throat. Panicking, Lila got to her feet. What had she done?

Maybe I wasn't meant to leave the school building at lunch, she thought nervously, following the secretary down the corridor. Had she broken a rule without realizing? She could imagine how well *that* would go down with her dad – especially this week. Josh must have told someone he'd seen her. But he wouldn't do that, would he? You never knew, with Josh. *If I'm not allowed on the beach in the day, then surely he isn't either,* she reminded herself, twisting her hands together as she reached the office door.

"Wait here, please," rapped the secretary.

She sank into a comfy chair. It probably wasn't Josh. But being called to the office was never good. She had learned that in London. She felt sick to her stomach. What more could go wrong?

FOURTEEN

The secretary reappeared with a frown on her face. Lila leaped to her feet, filled with dread.

"I don't know how it worked in London, Miss Murray," said the secretary coldly, "but at Heartside, the students don't have personal mail delivered to the school. Don't let it happen again."

Lila stared at the letter in the secretary's hand. She didn't understand.

The secretary waved the letter impatiently at her. "Aren't you going to take it?"

Lila took the letter. Her heart started to race at the familiar handwriting on the envelope. Lila Murray, 10Y.

"Thanks," she stammered. Her brain was bouncing

around like a ping-pong ball. Another note! What would this one say?

"Back to class now," said the secretary, and shut the office door.

Lila clutched the letter, feeling the grain of the paper between her fingers. Just holding it made her feel happy. She almost didn't want to open it and break the spell. Walking slowly back down the corridor, she turned into the girls' toilets and locked herself in a cubicle. Her fingers trembled as she prised open the flap.

You looked sad today. Don't be. Everything will work out.

Meet me at midnight on Saturday? There's a hidden cove in the cliffs, along from the main beach. Take the path by Kissing Island.

I'll be there waiting.

Lila's heart skipped at the thought of meeting her admirer on the beach. Surely it must be Ollie. Would it be a full moon tomorrow night? She almost swooned about how romantic that would be.

Thoughts of Ollie stayed in her mind. He wanted

to remember their first kiss. What could be more romantic than kissing on a secret beach at midnight? She folded the letter up carefully and tucked it back inside its envelope. If she was going to do this, it would require careful planning.

Lila paced impatiently in her bedroom on Saturday evening, waiting for the doorbell. When it rang, she took the stairs three at a time.

"Hey," she said breathlessly. "Come in."

Polly hefted her overnight bag over her shoulder. "Thanks for inviting me over. I haven't had a sleepover in ages." She looked over Lila's shoulder at the softly lit hallway. Everything had finally been unpacked. There were pictures on the walls, and a coat rack had been screwed into place beside the glass-panelled front door. A round wooden tub at the foot of the stairs held umbrellas and sticks and a few wellington boots. "Are your brothers going to jump out at me again?" she added, a little cautiously.

"They're out," Lila replied. "Dad's working. It's just me and Mum tonight." She dragged Polly inside.

"Come upstairs, I want to show you something."

When they reached Lila's bedroom, Lila pressed the latest note into Polly's hands.

Polly peered at the handwriting. "Your secret admirer again? What's that now – two notes?"

"Three," Lila confessed. She gave Polly the note she'd got two days earlier. "I'm sorry I didn't show you the second one. My head's been in a funny place this week, but I'm feeling better now. Things are clearer. What do you think?"

She waited as Polly read the notes.

"You're not going to meet him," Polly said disbelievingly, looking up. "Are you?"

Lila felt defiant. These notes were the best thing that had happened to her since she'd got to Heartside Bay. "Why not?" she challenged.

"Lila, that's not a good idea," said Polly in alarm. "In fact, it's a really BAD idea. You can't go out at midnight to meet a total stranger!"

"After Santiago called me yesterday, I was a mess," Lila groaned, throwing herself down on the bed. "It's as if the person writing these letters *knew* how I was feeling, and how to make me feel better. I feel sure I can trust him, Polly."

"Whoa, rewind," said Polly. "Who's Santiago?"

"My ex. The guy who's been texting me." Lila shot a cautious glance at her bedroom door. She didn't want her parents hearing this. "I spoke to him yesterday. He wants us to get back together. I said no. I got into a lot of trouble with him, back in London."

"Wow," said Polly. She laughed in amazement. "When you fell into class on the first day, you didn't look like a girl with secrets."

"Believe me, I have plenty," said Lila. "I have been bursting to tell you everything since I got the last note. Tell me honestly, Polly. Do you think it could be Ollie?"

Polly scoffed. "He's not the kind of guy who writes letters. He's more likely to sign a football."

"Maybe he's got a romantic side," Lila giggled.

"Unlikely," said Polly.

She was looking serious again. Lila wondered if she'd made her friend angry. Then she remembered that they still hadn't talked about what had happened on Wednesday.

"I'm sorry I kind of dumped you at the Heartbeat

Café," she said awkwardly. "It's just – I was feeling bad, and you were ages in the queue, and when Ollie signalled that he wanted to meet me. . ."

"Don't worry about it," Polly said. "Just promise you won't go and meet the letter guy tonight. It could be anyone. It could even be one of Eve's tricks."

Lila gnawed her lip. She hadn't considered the Eve angle. Meeting on the beach had felt like such a good idea when she first read the note. Now that Polly was pointing out the problems, she could see that maybe it was a little crazy.

Polly was right. She shouldn't go.

"I can't believe we're doing this," whispered Polly, unhappily.

Lila felt a rush of gratitude. "Thanks for coming with me." If she was honest, she felt a lot safer knowing Polly would be there too – particularly if this *was* one of Eve's traps. If it *wasn't*, well . . . the kissing would have to wait. Lila hugged herself as a thrill of anticipation ran through her.

They stepped out of the front door. A figure suddenly emerged from the shadows. Lila gasped. She would have known that silhouette anywhere. This wasn't happening. Not now!

Polly opened her mouth to scream.

"It's OK," Lila said quickly, before Polly woke up the entire street. She gazed at the tall, dark-haired boy in front of her with a mixture of pleasure and annoyance. "I know him."

Looking wide-eyed and frightened, Polly closed her mouth again.

Santiago was shivering in his thin coat, but his eyes sparkled with pleasure in the moonlight. "Hello, baby," he said in delight. "You don't know how good it is to see you."

"What are you *doing* here, Santiago?" Lila groaned.

"I needed to see you so badly. I caught a train as soon as you hung up this afternoon," he said. "I'm here to win you back, Lil. I will beg if I have to."

He was just as gorgeous as Lila remembered. A long dark lock of hair hung over one eye, and his teeth gleamed in the moonlight. For a moment, she forgot about her secret admirer, and her midnight rendezvous, and every single reason why she had left the house.

Upstairs, a light flicked on. Lila was shocked back to reality. If her mother looked out of the window now and saw her with Santiago . . . she would be grounded for life!

FIFTEEN

Lila dragged Santiago back into the shadows. Mistaking the reason for Lila's actions, Santiago pulled her towards him with his eyes gleaming.

"You have to leave," Lila hissed. Her gaze flicked fearfully to the upstairs window, where she could see her mother moving around. "Do you want my parents to kill me?"

"I don't care about them," he murmured, putting his arm around her shoulders again. His eyes smouldered, even in the moonlight. "I only care about you."

Lila exchanged an agonized glance with Polly. It was nearly a quarter to midnight. They would never reach the cove in time!

"Hi, Santiago, I'm Polly," said Polly. "I've heard all about you."

Now isn't the time to try and make friends! Lila thought. They had to get out of this mess. It would break her heart if Ollie stopped writing her letters because she didn't reach their meeting place in time.

Santiago looked pleased by Polly's interest. "I wish I could say the same. But Lil has been . . . *incommunicado*, shall we say?"

"Did you know that Heartside is famous for its beaches?" Polly went on.

We're running out of time! Lila mouthed frantically.

Santiago shrugged. "Of course."

"So," Polly went on, "why don't we continue this at the beach? It'll be great down there in the moonlight."

"Yeah," Lila agreed, realizing what Polly had in mind, "we can talk properly there."

Santiago shrugged. "OK."

"We follow the road that way," said Polly, pointing towards the town.

"Thanks," Lila muttered as Santiago nodded and set off down the street with his long, loping stride. He always reminded her of a wolf – and not only when he walked. Her legs felt wobbly with relief. "I owe you."

"Just call me your guardian angel," Polly answered. "What are you going to do if we get to the beach and the letter-writer's there? He won't be expecting three of us."

"Let's worry about that later."

They caught up with Santiago, who smiled at Lila and put his arm around her shoulders again. Lila tensed up.

"You are just as lovely as ever, Lil," Santiago murmured as they walked. "Your eyes are even bluer than I remember. Like sapphires."

You can't see the colour of someone's eyes by moonlight, Lila thought.

Glancing at Polly, Lila saw her friend was gazing steadfastly at the ground. Lila thought uncomfortably about how she had behaved with Ollie at the Heartbeat Café, and what she was doing now with Santiago, and the hundred or more rules she was breaking by being out so late. What did Polly really think of her? It was so hard to tell.

All these thoughts were pushed aside as they reached the beach. It did look incredible in the moonlight. The tide was out; the sand was a pearly grey and the tops of the waves hissed and broke in glittering bars across the dark horizon. Several wooden boats were moored on the beach, lying on the sand. Lila's eyes flicked wistfully towards Kissing Island. It would be wonderful to be standing on the shore of that little rocky outcrop, gazing into Ollie's eyes.

She sneaked a glance at her phone. Ten past midnight. Her heart plummeted like a stone. What if they were too late?

The feeling of loss was crushing. Tears of frustration blurred her eyes. What if the letter-writer had left the cove already, and appeared right now on the beach, and saw her with Santiago? He would never write her one of his wonderful notes again. She didn't think she could bear it.

Her eyes caught a flash of movement beside the rocks. She tensed. Was it just her imagination, or was someone there?

"I can see why this place is so famous," Santiago said, kissing her lightly beside her ear. "It's beautiful. But not as beautiful as you. You are my lucky star, Lil. I am nothing without you."

He moved closer, blocking her view of the rocks and whoever or whatever had been there. She felt irritated. "I love you, Lil," Santiago whispered.

His head dropped swiftly towards her, his lips seeking hers. And in that moment, she knew she felt nothing for him any more. Not a flicker, nor a spark. He was still romantic, and handsome, and impulsive – all the things that she had loved him for when they were in London. But it wasn't enough. Not any more. She didn't want to start lying to her parents again, ruining everything she was trying to achieve in Heartside Bay, just for him, particularly after what had happened. Her family had already given up so much because of her.

"Stop," she said, pushing him away.

"Didn't you hear me?" he said passionately. He pushed back his coat sleeve so she could see her initials on his wrist. "I did this because I love you. I want to be with you. I've come all the way from London for you, Lil. . ."

He wrapped his arms more tightly around her. For the first time, Lila felt worried.

"It's over, Santiago," she said. Her mouth felt dry.

"You don't know what you're saying." His face looked ghostly in the moonlight. "You can't deny the way we feel about each other!"

The hissing sounds of the moonlit sea gave her strength, encouraging her onwards.

"Go home, Santiago. There's nothing here for you any more," she said as gently as she could.

"I don't believe you," he said furiously. "Why are you saying this?"

He tried to kiss her for the second time. Lila pushed him backwards. Polly ran protectively towards her as Santiago tripped over a plastic float, almost losing his balance.

"I love you, Lil!" he shouted as he staggered upright again. "You can't reject me! I'll . . . I'll. . ."

He spun around, seized the hard plastic float he had stumbled against, whirled it around his head and brought it smashing to the ground. The float groaned and splintered at the force of the impact. Polly screamed.

"Santiago, stop!" Lila pleaded.

Ignoring her cries, he smashed a second float. Fragments of hard plastic rained around Lila and Polly as they cowered on the sand. Lila realized that he was crying.

Santiago suddenly ran at full speed towards the wooden boat moored nearby. He kicked the side of the boat so hard that his foot went through the boards.

"Stop. Please stop!"

Somewhere up towards the town centre, Lila heard sirens. The moonlit sky was suddenly striped with flashing blue lights as two police cars raced on to the beach, spraying sand through the air. Lila felt like she was waking from some terrible dream as her father climbed out of the first car. He saw Lila standing frozen amid a wreckage of floats and splintered planks, and she trembled at the shock and pain in his eyes.

"Dad. . ." she began falteringly. But what could she say?

Two officers had seized Santiago by the arms and

were pushing him, still struggling, into the back seat of the second car. Lila's dad tore his eyes from Lila and fixed them coldly on Polly, who was standing in Lila's shadow.

"None of this is Polly's fault, Dad," Lila said in desperation. "I had arranged to meet someone on the beach tonight, I admit it – but I swear I didn't arrange to meet Santiago!"

"You promised us you wouldn't see that boy again," said her father.

"I *didn't*—"

"You *swore*," her dad repeated. "And yet here you are, with him, causing trouble!"

"She's telling the truth, Chief Murray," said Polly tentatively. "Santiago surprised her tonight. None of this was Lila's fault."

Lila watched her father run his hands through his hair. "I want to believe you," he said wearily, "but I'm afraid I can't. Whether you arranged to meet that boy or not, Lila, you still sneaked out tonight without telling us where you were going – not to mention how you have embarrassed me tonight. This will go on record – my own daughter, mixing with troublemakers and disturbing the peace, all in the first week of my new job. What will my officers think? How am I supposed to deal with this?"

Tears stung Lila's eyes. She bowed her head.

"Your mother and I trusted you," he said harshly. "And you have broken our trust after everything we've done for you. You're grounded. You will hand over your phone, and you will come home straight after school every single day. Is that clear?"

Polly slipped her hand into Lila's and gave it a silent squeeze. Sniffing, Lila passed her phone to her dad. Her heart was in pieces. She had tried so hard to make a fresh start but she had ruined it.

"We will give your friend a lift back to her house," said her dad, regarding Polly with hard eyes. "And we will return her belongings in the morning. When we get home, you will go to bed. We will discuss this with your mother tomorrow. I won't have you waking her up and worrying her at this time of night."

The second car squealed away, carrying Santiago to the police station. Polly and Lila slid silently into the back of Lila's dad's car. With the grille dividing them from her father and the driver, Lila felt more like a criminal than ever.

Would her dad ever forgive her for this latest catastrophe? And had she ruined her chances with the letter-writer for ever?

SIXTEEN

On Monday, Lila was convinced everyone was staring at her, whispering about her. There was something about the way they glanced at her as she put her belongings in her locker, and how they gawped in the toilets, and laughed behind their hands in the classroom. Did they know everything?

"You're being paranoid," insisted Polly.

"I swear I'm not," said Lila unhappily. "Someone saw us in the squad car on Saturday night – or heard about it. This is a small town. Are you telling me kids get arrested on the beach every weekend?"

Polly wouldn't meet her eyes. "You're being paranoid," she repeated.

Lila rested her head on the cool surface of her desk. If only she was. Maybe if she wished hard enough, she could turn back time and undo the whole of Saturday night. Santiago's anger had scared her. He had always been passionate, but he had never been violent. She could still hear the crunching sound of his foot going through the wooden side of that boat. For the first time, she understood how dangerous love could be and how it could make you do crazy things. Santiago was living proof. Would she ever be ready for that kind of responsibility again?

The feeling that she was being talked about carried on through English and maths. Conversations stopped as she hurried past people on her way to the next class. There was a burst of mocking laughter as she turned the corner. She was so desperate to find her seat in history without catching anyone's eye that she accidentally stumbled over a chair leg. Josh caught her by the elbow.

"Steady," he said.

"Thanks," Lila muttered. She sat down, her ears burning as she imagined the conversations everyone would be having today. *A police car, and her dad the chief of police! Yeah, she was meeting a guy . . . he kicked a massive hole in the side of a boat. . .*

"Lila?"

Ms Andrews was looking enquiringly at her.

"Uh, yes?" Lila stuttered.

"Any ideas?"

Lila had no clue what the history teacher had asked her. She felt like a rabbit in the headlights of a large truck. As she floundered, Josh silently pushed a piece of paper towards her.

"The . . . blockade resulted in the creation of two states, West and East Germany," Lila read, barely taking in the meaning of the block letters neatly printed beneath her nose.

"Correct," said Ms Andrews. "The Federal Republic of Germany remained connected with the West, while the German Democratic Republic allied itself with the Soviet Union."

"Keep breathing," Josh advised in a low voice as Ms Andrews asked someone else a question. "All mammals require oxygen."

Underneath his quiet demeanour, Josh was kind of funny, Lila realized.

"Thank you," she mumbled.

"Any time."

He pushed his glasses up his nose and bent over his work. Lila wanted to keep talking to him. As a fellow outsider, Josh might understand a little of how she felt. "Not drawing today?" she fished, glancing at the closed sketchbook beside him.

"I need a new book; I finished that one earlier. You look terrible, by the way," he added, looking at her properly. "It's probably the sea air. People say it's good for you, but it actually gives you skin like a fish."

Lila snorted with laughter. A couple of heads turned towards her in surprise.

"You say the strangest things," she said, trying to straighten out her face.

He spread his hands. "What can I say? I'm weird."

This was her chance, Lila knew it.

"Josh," she said, seizing her courage with both hands. "What are people saying about me?"

He flushed. "Why are you asking me? No one tells me anything."

She noticed he hadn't answered her question. "You can tell me, it's OK. Is it about this weekend?"

The frown on his face was genuinely puzzled. "What happened this weekend?"

The blood drained from Lila's face. The whispering *wasn't* about this weekend? Then what. . .

"It's about why you moved to Heartside," Josh said.

Her stomach clenched in shock. She should have expected this, but after all the drama at the beach. . .

She grasped Josh's arm. "What are they saying?"

He looked so serious that she braced herself for the worst.

"Well, among other things, that you're a cat burglar who tried to rip off a footballer's house in Chelsea."

"What?" she said in astonishment. Had she heard right? A *cat burglar*?

Josh grinned. "My favourite rumour is that your parents adopted you because your real parents are connected to the mob. When someone found out who you were, your parents moved down here and changed your name. There's other stuff too, but it's nowhere near as interesting."

"They're seriously saying those things about me?" Lila said, amazed. "But that's insane!"

"Don't worry about it. The best thing to do is keep

your head down and your mouth shut. The vultures will move on to another victim sooner or later."

The tone of his voice gave Lila the strong sense that he was speaking from experience.

"If it makes you feel any better," he added, "I don't believe a word that anyone is saying. Although you do look kind of Italian," he added, with a quirk of his lips.

Lila laughed again, without thinking.

"Lila and Josh, a bit more concentration, please!" called Ms Andrews.

Lila found herself hoping that she and Josh could be proper friends. His take on life made her feel better about pretty much everything.

They walked to lunch together. Hearing everyone whispering didn't hurt Lila's feelings so much now. She just kept seeing herself in a cat burglar outfit, scaling the roofs of London. It was hard to feel upset with such a stupid image in her head.

Her mood was abruptly punctured as she set foot in the canteen.

"So, new girl," said Eve loudly, from a nearby table. "Is it true?"

The canteen hushed. Hundreds of eyes looked

at her. Lila was mortified. She could feel her heart banging against her ribcage. Should she take Josh's advice and ignore the question? Or was this her chance to put everything right? She glanced at Josh for help. He shook his head almost imperceptibly. Lila caught Rhi's eye next, sitting beside Eve. Her former friend looked at her steadily, her expression giving nothing away.

"Is what true?" she said, turning back to Eve as coolly as she could. "That I'm a cat burglar? Miaow. Or that I'm the love child of a mobster? *Ciao.*"

Food lay forgotten on the tables as several people laughed. Eyes swivelled from Lila to Eve and back again, as everyone waited to see what would happen next.

"Well now, aren't you funny," Eve drawled. She pushed her shining auburn hair back over her shoulders. "If there's no secret, you can tell us. All of us. Why did you leave London, Lila Murray? We're all ears."

Lila realized that she couldn't ignore this. Not any more. She didn't need any extra lies in her life. It was time to come clean.

SEVENTEEN

Before she could talk herself out of it, Lila hitched up her skirt and climbed on to one of the chairs surrounding Eve's table. Eve snatched her fingers away from the tabletop as Lila planted both feet in the middle of the table and waved to get the whole room's attention.

"What's she doing?"

"Is she *mental*?"

Whispers and roars of appreciative laughter swept through the room. Several teachers stood up with frowns on their faces.

Lila swallowed. *You're here now*, she said to herself, staring at the sea of faces avidly turned in her direction. *You'd better make this good.*

"My name is Lila Murray," she began. "There are

some rumours about me that are going around school at the moment. I can understand that. The new girl is always interesting." She was feeling a little dizzy at what she was doing.

"Personally? I find you very boring," said Eve in a loud, waspish voice.

There were a few sniggers, but Lila pressed on. "When I was in London, I made mistakes that hurt people. Big mistakes." She looked pleadingly around the room. "Everyone makes mistakes. Right?"

"Not me," someone shouted.

A few people cheered. Others made shushing noises, keen to hear what Lila had to say next.

"I've paid for those mistakes, and I've left them behind," she said. "Heartside Bay is a new start for me. I'm a different person now."

"A leopard never changes its spots!" someone called.

Lila's lips felt horribly dry. She licked them and tried to frame her next words as carefully as she could.

"You have a choice," she said bravely. "You can believe the rumours, or you can get to know me and find out the truth for yourselves. It's up to you."

"Get off that table!" Mr Morrison shouted, striding through the canteen. "This is a food hall, not a theatre!"

There was the sound of applause. Lila looked around to see Ollie with his hands above his head, clapping. Polly joined in, whooping and stamping her shiny brogues on the canteen floor.

Others started clapping now and stamping their feet. Before Mr Morrison had a total meltdown, Lila climbed off the table with trembling legs, hoping she wouldn't trip on anything on her way back to the floor. A few people patted her on the back; others nodded, or smiled, or looked thoughtful. Eve still had a sneer on her face, but Lila was more interested in the look on Rhi's face. She thought she could see tears in her old friend's eyes.

"Rhi," she said, feeling a wobble in her own voice. "I'm so, so sorry about the way I treated you in London. I was a total cow and I deeply regret it. Can you forgive me? After your—"

Rhi walked up to Lila and hugged her, stopping her from finishing her sentence.

"You're not the only one who wants to leave the past behind," she said, her voice muffled against Lila's shoulder. "Don't say any more, OK?"

"Very touching," sneered Eve, dragging Rhi away from Lila's embrace. "You know how to milk an audience, new girl – I'll give you that. But stay away from my friend. You've hurt her enough."

"But—" Lila began.

She felt a hand on her arm.

"That was quite a speech," Polly said, smiling.

Lila decided to try and find Rhi later. They had a lot to talk about. "Did I make any sense?" she asked Polly. "My head was spinning so much. . ."

"You sounded great," Ollie butted in. "Doing that really took some courage, Lila. It was amazing, what you just did," he said, in a husky voice.

Lila felt almost blinded by the admiration in his blue eyes. She glanced around for Josh, but as usual he had disappeared.

"So what did you do?" Polly asked after school. "In London, I mean?"

"I didn't rob any footballers," Lila said. She felt lighter than she had in weeks as they walked down the corridor towards the lockers. "I had a party that went wrong. Santiago's friends turned up and got really drunk. I lost control, the house was wrecked, and Dad nearly lost his job over it. It almost ended up on the news. It nearly ruined everything. That's why we moved here." She still felt a hot wave of shame at the thought of that night. But it really was behind her now.

"Something tells me you didn't polish your shoes or brush your hair quite as much as you do these days," Polly remarked.

Lila turned her head upside down and gave it a vigorous rub. Then she flipped her head back again, rumpling the top of her hair one more time. The curls and mess that resulted felt comfortable, and familiar. "I looked more like this," she said. "Only all over."

Polly laughed. Smiling, Lila opened her locker.

A note sat looking at her.

The secret admirer! was Lila's first tumbling thought. Had he forgiven her? She snatched up the note and unfolded it.

Sorry we couldn't talk earlier. Meet me at the end of the pier after school? Message me if you can't make it. Rhi xx

Lila stared at the number Rhi had scribbled at the bottom of the note. She didn't have her phone; it was in her dad's desk. She was supposed to go straight home after school, but she couldn't let Rhi down – not now they had turned such a major corner. Could she meet her and just get home a little later? There would be hell to pay. Without her phone, she couldn't warn anyone that she would be late.

Deciding it was worth a telling-off, Lila folded the note and put it in her bag.

"I have to go," she told Polly, whose head was deep inside her own locker.

"Sure," said Polly, pulling her head out again. "See you tomorrow. And Lila?"

"Yes?"

Polly grinned. "Well done again, for today."

It was blustery outside today, and bitterly cold. Lila walked as fast as she could, mindful that every minute would count. The road to the beach was getting more and more familiar these days.

She saw Rhi standing alone at the end of the pier several minutes before she reached her. Seagulls dived around Lila as she jogged the length of the old wooden boards, ducking to avoid the worst of the sea as it smashed loudly against the struts of the pier.

"Sorry about this," Rhi said, waving at the windswept pier. "It's kind of cold for a meeting place. But I didn't want anyone to overhear us."

Rhi's face had grown thinner since London, Lila thought. She could still see the grief in her old friend's eyes.

"I really am sorry about your sister," Lila said, feeling for the right words. "I didn't know what to say to you when she died. I should have been a better friend when you needed me."

Rhi smiled sadly. "We were kids," she said. "Like you said in the canteen, kids make mistakes. I made a mistake too. I told Eve what happened in London. I never thought she'd use it to turn the whole school against you the way she has."

"I can't believe you're friends with Eve Somerstown," said Lila. It was hard not to sound bitter.

"Eve has a good side to her," Rhi said loyally. "When I moved to Heartside, I was a grieving mess. She helped me a lot. She and you are the only ones who know about Ruth and the car accident. Like you, there are things I want to leave behind."

Lila frowned. Was Rhi trying to forget her sister?

"I'll never forget Ruth," Rhi said softly, as if she had read Lila's mind. "I think about her every day, and I miss her like a limb. But in Heartside, I want to be more than the girl with a dead sister. Do you know what I mean?"

"Yes," said Lila. She knew exactly what Rhi meant.

"Of course you do," Rhi nodded. "So how about I help you with your fresh start, and you keep my secret?"

"It's a deal," Lila promised.

They smiled at each other.

"Friends again?" Lila said hopefully. With Rhi, Polly, Ollie and Josh, she could start to feel at home in Heartside.

"I'd like that," Rhi said. "But with Eve around, that's going to be tricky." She shook her head. "You really walked into a wasps' nest when you went after Ollie."

"I didn't go after Ollie," Lila protested. "He came after *me*. And we can't help who we fall for."

Rhi pulled a face. "Eve doesn't see it like that. I'd like to be friends, Lila, and I'm glad you feel the same—"

She stopped. Through the crash of the waves, Lila heard the sound of footsteps on the boards behind her. She swung round. Eve was striding towards them, the smaller figure of Polly right behind her.

And Eve didn't look happy.

EIGHTEEN

Eve came right up to Lila and poked her hard on the shoulder. "Stealing my boyfriend not enough for you, so you thought you'd steal my friend as well?"

Now that she had made that speech in the canteen, and talked properly with Rhi, Lila felt powerful again. She flicked Eve's fingers off like flies. "I'll talk to whoever I like," she said coolly.

"I thought you had to go home straight after school, Lila?" said Polly from behind Eve.

Eve pulled out her phone. "I'm sure Daddy the police officer would be thrilled to know that his daughter is disobeying orders," she said with a nasty smile. "Let's call the police station and tell him."

A great wave of rage swelled up in Lila's heart. Eve

was the cause of so much that had gone wrong for her in Heartside. She lunged towards her. Eve tucked her phone away and curled her hands like a cat preparing to scratch. Polly jumped between them, waving her arms for calm.

"Stop it," said Rhi sharply.

It was the first thing she had said, and she said it with such authority that Lila, Eve and Polly all stopped in their tracks, and turned their heads, and fell silent.

"This is so *stupid*." Tears brightened Rhi's dark eyes. "Why do you have to fight? Life is too short for arguments about who's friends with who, and who's going out with who. I learned that the hard way when I lost my sister."

"I didn't know you lost a sister," Polly said, looking upset. "I'm sorry, Rhi."

Rhi dashed her tears away impatiently. "We don't have to be best friends," she said, looking at them all. "No one can click their fingers and make that happen overnight. But can't we just . . . get along?"

Lila lowered her hands. The red mist of rage was passing now. All she felt was embarrassment that she'd lost control like that, and let her feelings take over. She was no better than Santiago.

"I'm sorry," she said stiffly.

Eve tossed her head. "Whatever."

"I want to stop fighting too," said Polly, putting a tentative hand on Eve's arm. "Can we maybe call a truce as well?"

"Fine," Eve said, rolling her eyes. She looked at Lila again. "I'm *so* over Ollie, by the way," she said. "You're welcome to him, if dating rejects is your thing. I'm bringing a new guy to my party who makes Ollie look like a dumb little kid."

Lila felt awash with relief. It looked like she was getting somewhere with Eve at last. She felt a little jump of pleasure at the thought of Ollie, his bright blue eyes and the way he had looked at her in that smelly old bathroom. She didn't care whether he was a reject or not.

"We're still not friends, by the way," Eve added in a hard voice. Her eyes flickered a little. "But we're not enemies either. If Rhi can tolerate you, then I guess I can too."

The smile that broke over Rhi's face was like the sun coming out of the clouds.

"This is where we start again, OK?" she said happily. "Now let's go to the Heartbeat to celebrate our truce. I could really use a hot chocolate – I'm freezing."

The wind coming in from the sea was bitter. Lila was suddenly aware that she was almost wet through from the spray which had been thundering against the pier the whole time they had been talking. Hot chocolate at the Heartbeat sounded perfect.

They were almost there – Rhi arm in arm with Eve, Lila with Polly – when Lila stopped and groaned. "I can't come," she said. "I was supposed to be home half an hour ago!"

"What a pity," said Eve. "I'm sure we'll all miss your company."

"Eve," Rhi reminded her gently.

Eve puffed her fringe away from her face. Even in the damp air, her hair looked perfect. "OK," she said a little gruffly. "That was uncalled for."

Lila grinned. An almost-apology from Eve? That was a first. Maybe things would work out in Heartside after all. "Another time, maybe?" she said.

"Sure," Rhi promised with a warm smile.

Lila ran back towards the beach, and along the seafront to where the road curved up towards the cliff. As she jogged, she looked wistfully across the sand, towards Kissing Island and the start of the path to the secret cove. She still hadn't seen the cove for herself. *There will be other opportunities*, she told herself, getting a little breathless now as the road began to tilt uphill. Maybe even with a gang of friends. Unbelievably, it was starting to feel as if that might actually happen one day.

She suddenly stumbled over a stone and stopped. Shading her eyes, her heart thudding, she gazed back at the start of the secret path again. Ollie was standing there with his hands in his pockets. He was looking straight at her.

She couldn't decide what to do. She ought to go home; she was really late now, and if she didn't get back her dad would no doubt ground her for another week. Any kind of social life – especially one that might revolve around a secret beach – would be out of the window before it had even started. But she had to talk to Ollie too. Surely it wasn't a coicidence that he was standing exactly where she had seen – or thought she had seen – her secret admirer in the moonlight, beyond Santiago, on Saturday night? What should she do?

Dad'll kill me, she thought, racing back towards the beach with her heart fluttering in her chest. *But I have to know.*

"That's what I like to see," Ollie grinned as Lila stopped in front of him, panting, with her hands resting on her knees. "A beautiful girl running towards me like something from a movie."

He was looking particularly gorgeous, with the wind in his hair and his cheeks a healthy pink colour. The smile on his face told her how pleased he was to see her, and Lila's heart skipped.

Please be my letter-writer, she prayed to herself. She had never wanted anything so badly in her life.

"I've spoken to Eve," she gasped, straightening up and pressing her hand to her side. "She says she doesn't mind about you and me."

Ollie looked surprised. "How did you do that?"

"It wasn't me. It was Rhi."

Puzzlement replaced surprise on Ollie's face. "Rhi? Why would she get involved?"

"We go back a long way," Lila confessed. "Anyway, Eve says she's got someone else now."

Ollie pushed her flyaway hair away from her face.

"You're beautiful, Lila," he said. "I could gaze at you all day long."

The sun glimmered through the grey clouds, rich and orange as it settled towards the horizon. Lila's heart was so full she could hardly breathe. Ollie was coming closer. Was this it? Would this be the first kiss of true love? Would she one day stroll out to Kissing Island at low tide, hand in hand with Ollie?

His hands were cupping her face now, and he was drawing her towards him. Lila fizzed with anticipation, and lost herself in his shining blue eyes.

"Ollie," she said, feeling utterly breathless. "Is it you?"

"Is what me?" He was closer still.

"Are you my secret admirer?" she said in a rush. "I'm so sorry I never made it to our meeting on Saturday. I really tried, but—"

He pressed his finger against her mouth, and winked.

It *was* him. Lila knew it as surely as she knew the

feel of his hair beneath her fingers, short and soft and smelling of the sea. There was more to Ollie than just charm. He was a true romantic. She couldn't wait to be his girlfriend.

"I knew it was you," she breathed happily. "I knew it."

She closed her eyes, waiting for the feel of his lips at long last, pressing down on hers.

There was a shout. She opened her eyes in shock. Two figures had barrelled into Ollie from behind, and pushed him down in the sand.

NINETEEN

"Hey!" Ollie protested, struggling on to his feet. "What are you doing?"

He rushed at the two men who had pushed him over. Lila was frozen to the spot. It was only when she recognized Tim's green hoodie that she found her voice.

"NO!" she screamed, dashing between her brothers and Ollie. "STOP!"

"We have to sort out this scumbag first," Alex snarled, curling his fists. "He had his hands all over you!"

"Two against one," said Tim, in Ollie's face. "What are you going to do, mate?"

Lila was mortified. How could her brothers do this to her, at the most romantic moment of her life?

"I'll protect you, Lila," said Ollie angrily. "These two thugs don't scare me."

"You are so *dead*," Alex roared.

"He's my *friend*, you idiots!" Lila cried, shoving Alex backwards. *He'll never be anything else now*, she thought in agony. He wouldn't dare, the way her brothers were glaring at him. "Leave him alone!"

Alex paused, breathing hard. Tim hung back uncertainly while Ollie just looked confused.

"We've been waiting for you at home," Alex accused Lila with a jab of his finger. "You should have been back an hour ago. We were worried, so we came looking. And guess what we found?" He prodded Ollie meaningfully in the chest.

"You don't understand anything, Alex," Lila said through gritted teeth. She had never been so embarrassed in her life. "My friend will probably file for assault, the way you flew at him!"

"Who *are* these guys?" Ollie demanded, glaring at Tim and Alex.

"My brothers," Lila groaned. She wished she could just curl up and die. "The big idiot is Alex, and the small idiot is Tim."

"Pleased to meet you," said Tim. "And stay away from our sister."

"I'm really sorry you had to meet them at their worst," said Lila. She pushed her hair out of her eyes, and realized she was shaking. "You two owe Ollie an apology."

"It's OK," said Ollie shortly. He brushed the sand from his blazer, where he had landed on his back. "They were just protecting you. I guess they don't want you being with any guys."

"Glad you feel that way," said Alex.

Lila wanted to cry. Ollie would never kiss her now. She wondered how to make things right again.

"Thanks for looking out for me, Ollie," she said at last. She kissed his cheek, and tried not to remember how close she had been to kissing him for real.

"Sure," he said. He dug his fists into his pockets and gazed at the sand, looking confused.

"You're coming home now," Alex ordered, seizing Lila by the arm.

Lila shook him off. Her eyes filled with tears. "I'm not a dog," she hissed. "I can walk by myself, thanks."

Frustration and anger spilled out of Lila as soon as they were out of Ollie's sight.

"I hate you," she said passionately. "Both of you. I'm only coming because I don't want any more trouble."

"You've only been in this place for a week and already you've found a boyfriend," said Alex with a shake of his head.

I haven't! Lila wanted to shout. *And thanks to you two idiots, I probably never will!*

"He looked like a jock," said Tim. "You shouldn't trust jocks. They're not after your brains."

"How would you know, you total nerd?" said Lila bitterly.

"You can't go out with the first guy who shows an interest, Lil," said Alex. "You'll get a reputation."

Seething, Lila rammed her hands deep into her pockets and imagined doing dark and terrible things to both her brothers when they got home.

"At last!" said her mum, running down the stairs at the sound of Alex's key in the door. "Where have you *been*, Lila? You know the rules for this week. I have been crazy with worry!"

Lila looked at the white, pinched expression on her mother's face. A wave of remorse washed away her wallowing anger and resentment. Her mum only wanted what was best for her. She wanted her to be safe. Lila had caused them so much trouble already. It wasn't fair to start it all over again.

"I'm sorry," she said wearily. "It won't happen again."

She bowed her head and waited for her brothers to land her in it.

"Don't give her a hard time, Mum," said Alex. "Like some idiot tourist, she tried to find her way home through the Old Town, and she got totally lost. Without her phone she couldn't warn anyone that she was going to be late. We found her on the beach."

"Crying," Tim added helpfully.

Lila looked up, startled and wary. Alex gave her a little wink. All of a sudden, she didn't want to kick her brothers out to sea any more.

She saw her mother visibly relax. "Well, I suppose it's a little risky, sending you to school without a phone," she said. "The Old Town is like a rabbit warren. Maybe we should rethink that. I'll talk to your dad when he gets in."

"Good idea," said Tim.

Alex pinched Lila's cheek and wobbled it between his fingers. "That way, she'll never get lost again."

Lila's mother disappeared into her study, looking as though a great weight had been taken off her shoulders.

"Thanks," Lila muttered after a moment. She rubbed her cheek where Alex had pinched it.

"Any time," said Tim.

"But not too often," Alex warned.

Climbing slowly up the stairs to her room, Lila shut the door and leaned her head against the wall. *What a day*, she thought. It was a miracle she'd come through it alive. She dialled Polly's number on the landline. Polly answered at once.

"Hello?"

"Hi," Lila said, grateful to hear her friend's voice. "You won't believe the afternoon I've had."

She described how she'd seen Ollie on the beach after leaving the others outside the Heartbeat, and how close they had come to kissing, and how sure she felt that he was her secret admirer. But it was as if all the humiliation with her brothers had knocked the thrill out of it. And Ollie hadn't even said goodbye. "He's a superficial kind of guy," Polly said. "Ollie has about as much depth as a paddling pool, Lila. He can't help flirting with every girl he sees, except when he's kicking a ball around a muddy field, and then the ball gets all his attention. I really don't think he's the guy for you."

Lila felt surprised, and a little offended. Polly was being a bit harsh.

"He's not superficial," she said defensively. "You should have seen the way he stood up for me against my brothers."

"That doesn't mean the guy has any depth," said Polly. "Just a quick temper. Anyway," she added briskly, "I have news too. Eve's cousin Flynn was at the Heartbeat Café today. We used to hang out a couple of years ago, before he left Heartside for uni. So Flynn's been invited to Eve's Valentine's party, obviously, and we got talking when Eve went to the bathroom, and he invited me as his date! I don't like him particularly, but it'll really annoy Eve if I go."

So much for the truce, Lila thought. "I thought you and Eve made up today?"

"No chance," said Polly. "She pretended to be nice

to me in the café today, but I could tell she didn't mean it. She still hasn't invited me to her party. This will really wind her up."

"That's pretty cynical, Polly," said Lila. "I really want this truce to work, you know."

"Sorry," said Polly simply. "But I still don't trust her."

"Can't you even try?" Lila urged. "For Rhi's sake, if nothing else."

There was a pause on the other end.

"So you think I shouldn't go to the party with Flynn?" asked Polly reluctantly.

Lila rubbed her eyes. "I didn't say that."

"But what about the anti-Eve party we were going to have? Now you'll be on your own and—"

"I'll survive," Lila interrupted. "Don't miss out just because of me. I know you really want to go. I'll see you at school tomorrow, OK?"

"Sure," said Polly. Lila thought she sounded relieved. "See you in class."

She slumped on to her bed and closed her eyes.

TWENTY

On her way home after school on Wednesday, Lila paused on the corner of the pier. Eve was coming towards her, her auburn hair bouncing on her shoulders. Lila wondered if she should run away, or slide down an alleyway into the Old Town so she could avoid her. But Eve was waving and smiling, and Lila knew there was no escape.

Part of her was happy about it. She had learned from hard experience what it was like at Heartside High with Eve as her enemy, and her life was much easier now that the rest of the school had stopped ignoring her. Several kids had even started talking to her, prepared to take the challenge she had thrown at them in the canteen on Monday: to get to know her

159

for themselves. But the rest of her was cautious. Could it really be this easy? She couldn't help agreeing with Polly, that Eve was hard to trust.

The truce had held for two days now, ever since Rhi had laid down the law on the pier. Eve had moved from ignoring Lila to nodding at her, sometimes even saying "Hi." And smiling too. Lila couldn't get used to that. Every time Eve smiled in her direction, it felt like she was looking at a happy crocodile.

I will make this work, she thought firmly to herself as Eve broke into a light jog towards her. *Rhi is looking much happier this week. It's the least I can do for Rhi.*

"Hi!" Eve tossed her hair off her shoulders and adjusted the pink shoulder bag she was wearing. "I'm going to the police station now. Do you want to come?"

When Lila blinked in surprise, Eve gave a giggle. "I'm not in trouble or anything. I've just got something for your dad."

"I didn't think you knew my dad," Lila said.

Eve fell into step beside Lila. "I said hello at the Heartbeat Café, remember? Although this is actually from my father." She patted her shoulder bag. "We give out Valentine gifts every year for Dad's business connections and local VIPs. It's a Heartside tradition. Your dad counts as a VIP. Cool, don't you think?"

Lila wasn't sure how she felt about that. Her dad may have been the chief of police around here, but he was still just her dad.

"What's the present?" she asked, craning her neck to sneak a peek inside Eve's bag.

"Nosy," said Eve, her sharp side flashing through like a knife. She backtracked with a smile. "Don't spoil the surprise. You'll be able to see for yourself when we deliver it, won't you? My father counts as a VIP around here too. He's the mayor as well as one of this town's biggest employers, did you know?"

Lila shook her head.

"We do have a responsibility as one of the most influential families in the town to support local businesses. So we give out Valentines so that everyone feels valued," said Eve, airily.

If you're trying to intimidate me, it's working, Lila thought gloomily. The police station lay close to the high street, not far from the clock tower on the eastern edge of town. Lila walked with Eve along Marine

Parade, only half-listening as Eve chattered about life in Heartside.

"I know practically everyone along here," she said, waving at the shops and ice-cream parlours they were passing. "Their businesses need serious updating, though. My dad has plans for redeveloping this whole beachfront. It would be amazing if all the tenants would wake up and see the benefits of modernization. But they keep doing things the old way, like it's somehow better." She sighed. "No one glamorous will ever set up business in Heartside when it still looks like this."

Lila liked the way the old shops and parlours of Marine Parade looked, with their weatherboarded faces, old-style neon signs, curly metal balconies and gleaming lead-paned windows. But in the interests of the truce, she kept her mouth shut.

Eve pointed at a gleaming development perched up high on the cliffs ahead of them. Cranes bristled on the skyline. "My father's building that," she said. "It's a new shopping centre. He's going to build these amazing apartments with sea views up there too. He wants to build a marina to go alongside all of it.

Imagine if all those billionaire yachts you see in the Mediterranean started coming to Heartside! It would be amazing. Like St Tropez."

Eve's eyes sparkled at the thought of beautiful yachts being moored in the bay. For the first time, Lila saw something likeable about Eve. Suddenly, she understood why Rhi liked her. There was something about being with her that made anything seem possible.

"Hello," Eve said to the police constable on the reception desk in the police station. She put her pink bag on the counter and drummed her neatly manicured nails. "I'm here to see Chief Murray."

"Your name, miss?" grunted the constable.

"Eve Somerstown."

Lila noticed how the constable's expression changed at the mention of Eve's surname.

"Oh, and this is Chief Murray's daughter," Eve added, waving regally at Lila. "So, is he free?"

Two minutes later, Lila and Eve were ushered into the chief of police's office. Lila gazed around at the white walls, hung with photos of her father at different stages in his career. His office looked much the same as the one he'd had in London, only with a view of the cliffs and the sparkling sea.

Her father sat in a low-backed swivel chair, his hat perched in front of him on his desk. "This is a pleasant surprise, Lila," he said. "And Miss Somerstown too?"

Something in his tone suggested to Lila that their visit wasn't a pleasant surprise at all.

"Please call me Eve, Chief Murray." Eve didn't seem to have noticed the strange atmosphere. "My father sent me with a little Valentine's gift for you. Silly really, but it's a Heartside tradition at this time of year. I do hope you like chocolates?"

She pulled a tissue-wrapped box of confectionery from her bag and laid it expectantly on Lila's dad's desk.

"That's thoughtful, Miss Somerstown," said Lila's dad, "but I'm afraid I can't accept it."

Lila wondered why her dad was insisting on using Eve's surname. It sounded strange and old-fashioned. *Maybe that's how they always do things in police stations,* she thought. She felt embarrassed, and a little annoyed. First Polly, now Eve. Didn't her father want her to make friends? If everything Eve had told her was true, the Somerstowns were worth knowing in this town.

"Why ever not?" Eve said, sounding a little indignant.

"Police officers can't accept gifts, however kindly meant," Lila's dad replied. He pushed the chocolates politely but firmly back across the desk.

Eve's cheeks flared with two spots of colour. Lila found herself feeling sorry for the Queen Bee of Heartside.

"Oh," she said, looking upset. "I hadn't thought of it that way."

Placing his hat on his head, Lila's dad extended an arm, showing Lila and Eve back into the corridor. "Like I say, it was a nice thought," he said. "Lila," he added a little pointedly, "shouldn't you be heading home?"

"Oh, does Lila have to go home already?" Eve sounded genuinely disappointed. "I thought I could show her a few Valentine's Day preparations before the parade on Saturday."

Lila's dad looked reluctant. "My daughter knows the rules this week," he said.

Eve wrinkled her nose prettily. "Valentine's Day only comes once a year, Chief Murray. We treat it like Christmas in Heartside. Just for a while?"

Her father sighed. "You're to be home by five, Lila. Understood?"

"Sorry about my dad," Lila told Eve as they left the station. She felt she had to explain. "I'm supposed to head straight home after school. Strict parents, you know?"

"Poor you," said Eve. "Oh well, an hour's better than nothing. Do you know about our Valentine's Day Festival on Saturday?"

Lila had seen the banners, and the street paintings, and heard the love songs on the town speakers. Valentine's Day was hard to miss around here. "Kind of," she said.

"You have to see the floats – they're really gorgeous," said Eve. She broke out the box of confectionery intended for Lila's father and put one in her mouth. "So are these," she added with a laugh. "Your dad's missing out."

The light was starting to fade from the sky now, and the streetlights were flickering on in a string of pink down the high street. They shared the chocolates, and Lila let Eve drag her behind the high street to a wide car park where a row of fantastically decorated floats stood under cover, ready for Saturday's festival. They were festooned in hearts and cupids, lips and ribbons and every possible thing vaguely connected with love. Lots of people were working on their floats in the lamplight, scrubbing the wheels of the vehicles, adjusting banners and layering on fresh swags of glitter and ribbon. The cheerful chatter and the smell of paint hung heavy in the air. Lila couldn't help relaxing, and allowed the romance of it all to soak into her skin. It was impossible to remain uneasy, surrounded by this many symbols of love and happiness. She couldn't help thinking of Ollie. What did he make of all of this?

"On Saturdays this place turns into a great big market," Eve told her. "It's especially good when Valentine's Day falls on a Saturday, like this year. You'll be able to buy *everything* to do with love – everything except a boyfriend." She giggled. "Believe me, I've tried."

Lila felt something close to happiness as she

laughed at Eve's daft joke and helped to finish off the chocolates. She was starting to believe that Eve was warming to her after all.

"And then of course there's the Valentine's Surprise," said Eve. "The kids leave a secret message for the town every year. It's a rites-of-passage thing. Rhi and I will probably do it together."

Lila pictured a great loveheart made out of rose petals on the beach, or a banner covered in kisses draped from the top of the clock tower. "That sounds really fun," she said eagerly. "Can I help?"

Eve considered it. "It's probably best if there's just two of us," she decided. "Maybe you could take Rhi's place this year."

The clock tower struck five.

"I have to go," said Lila regretfully.

Eve sighed. "Look, if you're interested in doing the Valentine's Surprise, meet me tonight on the cliff. There's a little cave just above the secret cove where we have parties in the summer. You'll know it when you see it. Shall we say midnight?"

Midnight? Why was everything always at midnight in this town?

Eve's eyebrows arched at the look on Lila's face. "Chicken?"

Lila felt scared at this flicker of the old Eve. "No!" she said defensively.

"Good," said Eve, relaxing. "So I'll see you there. And remember – don't tell anyone, or it'll ruin the surprise."

She waved carelessly over her shoulder, dropped the empty confectionery box in the bin and sauntered out of sight. Lila headed slowly in the opposite direction.

If she didn't meet Eve tonight, she'd be back at square one, she thought miserably. It had been such a relief, this afternoon, not having to worry about anything. But now the old nagging feeling was back. But could she really risk her parents' wrath twice in one week?

If she let Eve down this time, she knew she wouldn't get a second chance. And her life in Heartside would be over if Eve took against her again.

She had to risk it.

TWENTY-ONE

It was hard, concentrating on her homework that night. Lila did her best, working through the problems and trying to ignore the little voice in her head that kept asking the same question over and again.

Should she meet Eve at midnight? Could she risk it? Or was it the worst idea she'd ever had?

If she hadn't already been in trouble for her midnight meeting on the beach last weekend, she would do it in a blink. Life at Heartside would be too difficult to do anything else. She shuddered to think about how she would survive if Eve went back on the warpath.

She saved her work and glanced absently at the

clock on her wall. Her stomach flipped with terror. It was nearly eleven o'clock. She had to make a decision. Surely two midnight meetings couldn't go wrong in the same week?

As she chewed her nails and agonized about what to do, a message popped up on her screen.

Ollie: Hi Lila. Free to talk?

Lila had a flash memory of Ollie's face smiling down at her on the beach on Monday, on the point of kissing her. She'd seen him in school, of course, and she knew that he wasn't mad at her, but they hadn't managed to meet up properly because of Lila's curfew.

Lila: Hey. Just finished my homework. You?

Ollie: Footie practice and pizza. Homework not so much. Meet tomorrow?

Lila's fingers hovered over the keypad as she wondered what to say. Before she could decide, another message appeared.

Ollie: I want to pick up where we left off on Monday.

Lila's stomach squirmed pleasurably. How could she resist this guy? Grinning to herself, she typed a flirty reponse.

Lila: I don't know what you mean. . .

She felt as if she had hardly pressed send before his answer came winking back at her.

Ollie: Looking forward to refreshing your memory!

There was a knock. She slammed her laptop shut. *Why am I feeling guilty?* she wondered as her bedroom door opened. *I'm only talking to a friend!* But she knew her guilt was nothing to do with Ollie. It was because she had decided she would meet Eve.

"You should think about putting your light out now," said her mother.

"Just finishing some homework," Lila answered, crossing her fingers under her desk.

Her mum yawned, covering her mouth with her hand. "Can it wait until tomorrow? You have the whole weekend."

"Five more minutes," Lila promised.

When her mother had gone, Lila reopened her laptop.

Ollie: You still there?

Lila: Sorry, Mum came in. Listen, I have to be somewhere in forty mins. Can we talk tomorrow?

Ollie: Where are you going at this time of night?

Should she tell him? Eve had warned her to keep the Valentine's Surprise a secret. She limited herself to:

Lila: Tell you when I see you.

Ollie: When's that?

Lila: Tomorrow night?

Ollie: Can't. Party of the century, remember?

Lila grimaced. Eve's Valentine party. She'd forgotten about that. She felt a flash of hurt as she remembered the fun she thought she'd had with Eve that afternoon. Eve might talk to Lila now, but she still didn't like her enough to invite her to her party.

Her reply was a little waspish.

Lila: Lucky for some.

He'll probably kiss someone else at the party anyway, she thought irritably, shutting her laptop before he could reply. Polly had told her how people always got together at Eve's Valentine's parties. Even Polly was going with Eve's cousin Flynn, she remembered with a groan. All of a sudden, she felt lonely. There was nothing worse than knowing about a party but not being able to go.

She pulled on her darkest clothes and slid her phone into her pocket. Switching off her light, she waited for sounds from her parents' room to stop before tiptoeing down the stairs, grabbing a scarf and sliding out of the front door.

With only herself to worry about, the walk to the beach was surprisingly quick. There wasn't much moon, but the town glittered with Valentine's lights and it wasn't hard to see where she was going. She swung around the corner, up past the building site Eve had pointed out earlier that day, the cranes lit with festive garlands of blazing pink bulbs.

Why am I even meeting Eve if she can't be bothered to invite me to her party? Lila wondered, feeling strangely annoyed with herself. She knew it was stupid, wanting to be liked this much. But maybe she'd get an invitation after they had finished the surprise. Maybe Eve was just waiting to see if she would chicken out of tonight before telling her she could come.

Quickening her pace as she thought about the sparkly invitations, Lila found herself on top of the cliff in no time at all. She found the path Eve had mentioned straight away, leading off the road at a shallow angle and twisting back on itself as it led down the side of the cliff.

It was darker off the road. Halfway along, the path

flattened into a wide, open stretch of ground beside a wide cave mouth. Eve looked round at the sound of Lila's footsteps. Wiping her forehead, the spray can still in her hand, she grinned. "Glad you could make it, new girl," she said. She waved the spray can. "Want to give me a hand?"

Lila stared at the writing. Eve had got as far as HAP, the letters stretching up the smooth cliffside in long red gashes. Graffiti? She hadn't been expecting this.

"Don't look so scared," Eve scoffed. "It's only paint. It'll wash off in the next rainstorm. Your turn. It's P next."

Lila felt nervous as she stared at the can Eve had pressed in her hand. Even on her worst day, she had never damaged property, or scrawled messages on walls.

"Are you sure this is OK?" she said.

Eve laughed. "Kids around here do it all the time." She pointed at the faint marks scrawled on parts of the cliff. "It's practically expected on Valentine's Day. Different rules apply on Valentine's Day in this place."

It must be OK if Eve's doing it, Lila thought. But she still couldn't bring herself to raise the can, or direct the nozzle at the cliffside.

Eve made a tutting noise, patting the pockets of the thick downy jacket she was wearing. "I hid the rest of the paint in another cave further down the cliff. Back in a minute."

"Wait!" Lila said in dismay, but Eve had already gone.

Now what? Lila shivered a little, and looked at the paint can in her hand again. Should she start spraying without Eve? Something about this whole set-up was making her nervous. What should she do next?

She almost jumped out of her skin at the sound of footsteps on the path above her.

"I wasn't doing anything!" she said, dropping her spray can in panic. "I. . ."

"Thought I'd find you here," Ollie said, stopping by the cave. His blond hair glimmered in the faint moonlight.

Lila stared at him in disbelief. "What. . . How. . ."

Ollie bent down and picked up the can of paint. He waggled it at Lila. "Did Eve tell you to carry on spraying without her, by any chance?"

She nodded dumbly, unable to get her head around

seeing Ollie here, in the half-darkness, with the crashing sea the only sound for miles.

"How did you know I'd be here?" she managed. "I didn't tell you!"

Ollie sighed. "I've lived in Heartside Bay a long time. I know Eve better than she knows herself. She did this before, with another new kid at school. When you said you had to be somewhere in forty minutes. . . Well, forty minutes made it midnight, by my calculation. Most of Eve's tricks happen around midnight, in hidden places like this one. If you hadn't been at this cave, the secret cove would have been the next place to look. She's very predictable."

"But we made a truce!" Lila's eyes blurred with tears. "Why would she do something like this?"

"I'm sorry to tell you, but there is no truce," Ollie said gently. "She's only pretending, to keep Rhi happy. As usual, Eve has her own agenda."

Lila struggled to make sense of what Ollie was telling her.

"I got suspicious when you told me she'd said she was fine about you and me," Ollie continued. "There's no way she'd be fine about that. She's not the forgiving kind. Like I said, I know Eve pretty well."

Lila was trying to decide if she was upset or angry about Eve's trick when Ollie aimed the paint nozzle at her with a grin. "Fancy a paint fight?" he said teasingly.

It was difficult to brood on Eve when Ollie was grinning at her like that, the spray can levelled at her like a weapon.

"Don't you dare," Lila gasped, half-laughing as she raised her hands.

Ollie sprayed the paint in the air with a hissing sound. Lila gave a half-scream and started running. *Thank goodness for Ollie*, she thought, giggling madly as she legged it past the cave and down towards the beach. Without him, this evening would have been a complete disaster.

A warm arm wrapped around her middle and brought her crashing down.

"Got you," Ollie laughed, pinning her to the sandy ground. "No one escapes the paint monster."

Lila was breathless, and not just from running. His face was inches away. As they stared at each other, Ollie's expression changed. Gently, he brought his lips towards hers. Lila's heart pounded. She started to close her eyes.

On the road above the cliff path, Lila heard the telltale sound of wailing police sirens. She pushed Ollie away and jumped to her feet, her gut twisting in terror. It was like a horrible replay of Saturday night. Surely Eve wouldn't have. . .

"And Eve's revenge is complete," Ollie said, dusting himself down swiftly as he confirmed Lila's worst fears. "The perfect finishing touch. The police, finding you here with a can in your hand and three letters a mile high on the cliff? We have to get you out of here."

Lila was too shocked to resist as Ollie grabbed her hand and dragged her on down the path. They were running fast, her feet sliding on the pebbles and sand beneath her feet. Thank goodness she was wearing dark clothes. Thank goodness there was so little moon.

On the wind, Lila caught some of the police officers' conversation above their heads.

". . .tip-off . . . vandalism. . ."

Ollie pulled her onwards. They reached the secret cove, a half-moon shape among the rocks with the sea lapping gently at its shore. Eve was nowhere to be seen.

"You're a hero, Ollie," Lila gasped as they sprinted across the sand towards the path that she guessed would lead them to the main beach and safety. "You just saved my neck."

"Thank me by being my date at Eve's party tomorrow," Ollie panted back at her, over his shoulder. "What do you reckon?"

Eve will go mental, thought Lila. It was the best idea she'd heard in ages.

"You're on," she said.

Even to her own ears, her voice sounded like the clash of steely swords. This was war. She would never allow herself to be bullied by Eve Somerstown again.

TWENTY-TWO

Ollie walked her home. As they turned up her dark street, he slipped his hand into hers. Lila shook her head very slightly, pulled back and stuck her hands in her pockets instead. Sneaking through the streets with her heart in her mouth, waiting for police officers to jump out of the shadows and arrest her for damaging the cliff, had killed her appetite for romance. Now wasn't the right time. She wondered a little glumly if there was ever going to be a right time for her and Ollie.

You can kiss him at the party, she told herself. *Right under Eve's nose.*

A flare of pleasure went through her at the thought. Then she felt guilty. Did she want to kiss Ollie purely to annoy Eve?

"Are you going to be OK?" he asked as they drew up outside Lila's house.

Lila pulled herself out of her puzzling thoughts. "I'll be fine," she assured him. "Thanks. For everything." She shivered a little, thinking of how her evening could have turned out without Ollie's assistance.

"I guess now isn't the time for that kiss?" he asked hopefully.

Lila gazed into his eyes. They were hard to read in the darkness. "All I can think about right now is how mad I am at Eve," she said honestly. "I don't want to kiss you thinking like that."

He rocked on his toes and gazed at the ground. Lila wondered anxiously if he was going to say he'd changed his mind, that he didn't want to take her to the party after all. In that moment, she realized how badly she wanted to go. She hadn't been to a party in such a long time. She didn't care that her worst enemy was the host. She was just desperate for music, and dancing, and fun.

"Pick you up tonight at seven?" he said at last, looking up again.

Lila's heart steadied with relief. "Tonight?" she said, suddenly confused.

"It's past midnight," he pointed out. He smiled at her. "Happy Valentine's Day, Lila."

He touched her cheek lingeringly, then walked away with his head tucked down into his jacket. Part of Lila wanted to run after him. The rest kept her feet rooted to her front path.

There'll be time for kissing later, she reminded herself, letting herself in as quietly as she could.

She avoided the squeaky stair, and tiptoed into her bedroom with a sigh of relief. All of a sudden, she felt exhausted. It was all she could do to take off her shoes and collapse beneath her duvet.

"You want to go to a party tonight, with a boy? Do we know him?" said her dad the next morning with a heavy frown. Until half an hour ago, Lila's dad had refused to even consider letting her go to a party.

"We've only been in Heartside Bay for two weeks, Greg," Lila's mum pointed out. "Of course we don't know him. But we all have to start somewhere. Whose party is it, love?"

"Eve Somerstown." Lila had to repress a shudder as she said Eve's name. "You met her at the police station the other day, Dad."

"I know who Eve Somerstown is," said her dad. Lila thought he sounded grim. "And everyone at your school is going?"

"Pretty much." Lila bit into her toast and crossed her fingers tightly under the table.

"Fine," her father sighed. "But you're to be home by eleven, and I want to meet this date of yours before you leave. This is your chance – don't mess it up."

Lila wanted to shout with excitement. She was going to the party of the year, and there was nothing Eve could do about it.

"You will," she said breathlessly. "He's picking me up tonight at seven. I'll make sure he says hi. Thanks, Dad!"

She put her breakfast things in the dishwasher, planted a kiss on her father's bristly cheek and dashed for the stairs. She had an outfit to plan.

Two hours later, every item from her wardrobe lay scattered on the floor. Lila bit the side of her thumb, trying to work out what to wear. She had to look *amazing*. That way, her revenge on Eve would be complete.

And I want to be a date that Ollie will feel proud of, she reminded herself.

Another hour passed as she tried on everything she owned. Nothing was right.

"Need some help?" her mother asked, putting her head around the door.

"Yes," Lila groaned. "Can we go shopping?"

"What about this?"

Lila stared at the dress which had unfurled in her mother's hands. Made of some kind of crumply gold fabric, it shimmered like a living thing. It was strapless, with a fitted bodice and a short tulip-shaped skirt. She couldn't take her eyes off it.

"It's amazing," she breathed. "Where did you get it?"

"I wore it to parties thirty years ago. I think this kind of thing is trendy again, isn't it?"

"Don't use the word trendy, Mum," Lila advised. She took the outfit very carefully and held it up to the light. "It makes you sound seriously old."

She wriggled into the dress, sucked her breath in so her mum could pull up the zip at the back – and stared at the vision in her wardrobe mirror. She hardly recognized herself. Her waist nipped in like a model's. She was all legs, and her hair seemed to flash with gold highlights that she never knew she had.

"It's amazing!" she squealed, spinning on the spot. "And I can wear it? Really?"

"Take care of it." Her mum looked misty-eyed. "I have good memories of that outfit."

Lila was already imagining the make-up she would wear to maximize the glamour of the golden dress. "Mum, you're the best!"

With a dress like this, she thought ecstatically, *I plan to have some good memories of my own tonight!*

The doorbell rang at seven o'clock exactly. Smoothing her hair one more time and trying to control the flutters in her stomach, Lila opened the door.

"Whoa," said Ollie. Putting his hands on his heart, he pretended to stagger backwards. "I came to pick up Lila Murray, not an angel. You look *incredible*."

"Thanks," said Lila shyly. "You look pretty good yourself."

"What, this old thing?" He batted his eyelashes, smoothed down the front of his white dinner shirt and straightened his dark grey bow tie. He looked incredible.

Lila's dad loomed in the hallway behind her, and looked Ollie up and down. "We met at the Heartbeat Café, I believe."

Lila cringed, but Ollie was unfazed.

"I remember, Chief Murray. I'm Oliver Wright. Pleased to meet you again."

Looking mollified at Ollie's good manners, Lila's dad shook his hand. Lila felt an immense wave of relief.

"We'd better go," she said, and grabbed Ollie's hand to tow him down the path.

"Back by eleven, Lila," her dad called, and gently shut the door.

Lila stopped at the gate and gaped at the long black limousine parked across the road.

"That's never for us," she said in astonishment.

"Of course it's for us," said Ollie, pulling her

across the road. He opened the passenger door with a flourish, and Lila was assailed by the smell of polished car leather. "This isn't any old party, you know. Come on, or we'll be late."

Eve's driveway was lit by flaming torches. Sinking into the leather seats of the limousine, Lila could only stare at the expensive cars parked in front of the porticoed house, whose pink-lit columns looked like vast candy canes.

"Glad we didn't walk now?" Ollie enquired, opening the limo door.

Not trusting herself to speak, Lila simply nodded. Wriggling out of the limousine, she stood up, clutching her purse to her stomach. She could hear strains of music coming from inside the house, and the drone of chatter. She tried not to gawp at the white-gloved waiters standing by the door with trays full of glasses of sparkling punch.

Eve may be a cow, but one thing is clear, Lila thought as she and Ollie joined the crowd ascending the front steps. *She knows how to throw a party.*

Ollie showed the bouncer his sparkling pink ticket, and they were waved through.

"Great work," said a voice by Lila's elbow as she took a celebratory glass of punch.

Looking round, Lila saw a red-haired boy who looked faintly familiar. "What?" she asked in confusion.

The boy lowered his voice. "Your stunt at the cliff. Everyone's talking about it."

"I didn't—" Lila began.

"Who's been spreading that around?" Ollie cut in sharply.

"Everyone knows," said the boy, looking surprised at Ollie's tone of voice. "But don't worry, it's cool." He looked at Lila again. "Want to dance later, graffiti girl?"

"She'll be dancing with me," Ollie snapped, and the boy lifted his hands and melted into the crowd.

The punch tasted like acid in Lila's mouth. Eve's stunt may not have worked, but it looked as if the Ice Queen wasn't finished with Lila yet.

"I think we should go," she said in a low voice to Ollie.

"And let Eve win?" he said. "Come on. We're nearly inside."

The crush of people opened up into a large front hall swagged with red garlands and pink lights, filled with girls in glittering dresses and boys in tuxes. The hairs on the back of Lila's neck rose as every single person turned and stared at her.

They're staring at the graffiti girl, she thought, and felt hollow with misery.

Ollie set his empty glass down on a passing waiter's tray. "Let's get another drink," he said firmly.

It was easier said than done. Lila found herself surrounded before they could reach the bar.

"Awesome," said a girl in a full-length purple dress. "Is it true the police turned up?"

"You have nerves of steel, Lila," said someone else, and Lila was surprised that they knew her name.

"I . . . thanks, but it wasn't . . . I didn't. . ." she tried.

The crowd was having none of it.

"Dance with me later?" said a boy she'd never seen before.

"There's a party at mine next week," said the girl in purple. "You should come?"

Gradually it dawned on Lila that no one was

laughing at her. No one was turning away from her in disgust. Vandalism was a dumb thing to be admired for – she still felt guilty about the cliff, even though she hadn't lifted a finger to paint those letters – but it was nice to feel admired anyway. Something told her Eve hadn't planned it this way.

"What's she doing here?"

Lila met the glittering, angry green gaze of the party host herself. Eve was dressed in a cascade of pale blue sequins, her rich red hair caught up on top of her head with aquamarine drops at her ears. She truly was the Ice Queen of Heartside tonight.

"I don't recall inviting you," Eve said, running her eyes over Lila's dress with what Lila recognized, with some satisfaction, as envy.

"She's my date, Eve," said Ollie.

Eve flinched but swiftly recovered. "We don't have vandals here," she said sweetly. "Everyone knows about your ridiculous Valentine's message, Lila. They're laughing about you all over town."

"I don't see anyone laughing," said Lila coolly. "Do you?"

Eve's gazed flicked around the room. Groups

of people were watching Lila with interest. Several raised their punch glasses in her direction, in silent congratulation. Lila saw Eve's pale-blue manicure flex and curl into her palms.

"Someone get Security," she called, loud and imperious. "This person is leaving."

TWENTY-THREE

Colour rushed to Lila's cheeks. Of course Eve would throw her out. Why hadn't she thought of that? Suddenly she wished she hadn't chosen such a visible outfit. If she had turned up in something less eye-catching, this wouldn't be such a visible humiliation.

"You can't do that, Eve!" said Ollie indignantly. "She's *my* guest."

"And she's in *my* house," Eve hissed. She looked at Lila like she was a piece of gum stuck to the bottom of her pale blue, high-heeled shoe. "I can have who I want in my own house. Don't you agree?"

Lila was aware of a flash of colour appearing on her left.

"Leave her alone, Eve."

Polly was wearing what looked like something from the nineteen fifties, a vintage floral taffeta dress with a wide skirt and a cloud of stiff net petticoats over a pair of neat red-heeled shoes, with red lipstick to match. The red stripe in her hair gleamed with a coating of sparkle spray. She looked amazing.

Eve was pale with rage. "What is this, gatecrasher day? I didn't invite you to my party either, Polly Nelson."

"She's with me," said the red-haired boy Lila had met outside. *No wonder he looked familiar*, Lila thought distractedly. *He must be Eve's cousin, Flynn.*

Eve curled her lip. "Even my own family stabs me in the back, I see." She glared at Lila again. "I don't invite *vandals* to my house."

"Give it a rest, Eve," said Ollie, rolling his eyes. "I was there. I know what really happened."

Eve's pink-painted mouth worked like a goldfish. "I . . . *she* sprayed the cliff, Ollie," she said, trying to recover her poise. "She's just trying to prise you away from me. I don't know what she's told you, but you can't trust—"

"He can trust his own eyes," Lila interrupted. "It was a mean trick, Eve. And it's backfired on you, big time."

Rhi joined in, looking incredibly elegant in a long, red silk jumpsuit. She was holding hands with Max, whose all-black ensemble made him look like a well-dressed spy. The hurt in Rhi's wide dark eyes made Lila tremble.

"You *promised*," Rhi reminded Eve softly. "You said you'd leave Lila alone. Did what we said on the pier mean nothing to you?"

Eve's gaze flickered. "Of course it meant something."

"And yet here you are, Eve," said Max, putting his arm around Rhi's shoulders, "trying to ruin things for everyone else, as usual."

Eve made a hissing sound of frustration. Lila half-expected her to stamp her foot like the bad fairy in a fairytale.

"If Lila goes," said Ollie, "we go too." He looked round at the little group, his eyebrows raised. "Right?"

"Right," said Rhi, her eyes still fixed on Eve.

"If Rhi goes, I'm right behind her," Max agreed.

He pushed back his thick dark hair with his free hand. "And believe me, I'll make plenty of noise about it."

"Me too," said Polly cheerfully.

"I'm with her," said Flynn.

Lila realized that the room had gone very still. Two large security guys were making their way through the crowd, muscles bulging through their black shirts. One of them was fiddling with an earpiece. Conversations had stopped as everyone in the room avidly watched the drama unfold.

"So, Eve," said Ollie, folding his arms as the bouncers bore down on them. "What are you going to do?"

There was a moment of frozen nothing. Then Eve lunged towards Lila. Lila stepped back hastily, wondering if punching the party host was a really bad idea. She felt Eve's arms come round her. To her astonishment, two loud air kisses rang out of either side of her face.

"Lila darling, there's no need to look so petrified," Eve giggled, stepping back and patting her hair carelessly. The bracelets on her slim wrists jangled. "Sorry, boys," she said as the bouncers stopped beside her with enquiring looks on their granite-like faces. "It was a joke that got a bit out of hand. Of course Lila's staying. She's one of my besties." She waved at the watching crowd. "The show's over, darlings. Time to get this party started."

Lila flinched as Eve's arm snaked around her and squeezed her shoulder as if to prove the "besties" remark. The security guys gave businesslike nods and melted back towards the front door, and the general buzz of conversation started up again.

Holding her head high, Eve stalked away without another word. Lila rubbed at her shoulder. She could still feel Eve's cool fingers digging into her skin.

"Great party," said Max. "Really excellent vibes."

Ollie laughed. It broke the tension, and after a moment, Rhi and Polly laughed too. Max chuckled and rolled his eyes at the ceiling.

"Don't mind Eve," he told Lila with a flash of his white grin. "She's a little pussycat."

"With claws to match!" Polly said a little unsteadily. "I can't believe we got through that unscathed."

A burst of music suddenly broke through the chatter. Lila blinked at the gravelly tones of a certain unmistakable song issuing from a large room beyond the hallway, which, judging from the pretty pink sparkling lights, was hung with a glitter ball. Groups of people started heading for the music, chattering at full volume, while Lila listened in astonishment.

"That's not who I think it is," she said at last. "Is it?"

"One Direction! I think we might have struggled to get a better band for our anti-Eve party," Polly giggled, her eyes sparkling with excitement. "Don't you?"

Lila felt Ollie take her hand.

"Dance with me," he said softly, and dragged her towards the music.

Lila knew without a shadow of a doubt that this was going to be one of the best evenings of her life. She had never seen such beautiful party decorations, or lighting, and she had certainly never enjoyed a party where real-life rock stars made up the entertainment, nor worn such a perfect dress. She was light-headed with magic. Her argument with Eve paled into nothing as she laughed and flirted and jumped around the low-lit dance floor with *her friends*. They really were her friends, at last.

"Glad you came?" Ollie shouted in her ear as the room erupted at the start of a fresh, totally familiar tune.

"So glad," Lila shouted back, twirling around with Polly, her tulip-shaped skirt floating upwards like the petals on a golden flower.

"Your date's quite a mover, Ollie," said Max. He was dancing with his cheek pressed up against Rhi's. "She makes you look like an elephant."

Lila threw her arms into the air, loving the feel of her hair swishing across the top of her bare back. "I've always like elephants," she teased.

Ollie made a trumpeting noise and galloped around Lila and Polly. Lila giggled hopelessly, leaning on Polly for support.

Abruptly the music changed to a slow song. Half the floor dispersed, grumbling about slow dances, while the rest began to dance in couples, their eyes closed and their arms around each other's backs.

"Shall we?" said Ollie, smiling into Lila's eyes.

"As long as you don't tread on my toes, Dumbo," she said, smiling back.

She snuggled into his arms, enjoying the feel of his cheek against hers. His arms encircled her and his fingers stroked her bare back, while his face, eyes bright and intent, came closer. *Any moment now*, she thought in ecstasy.

"Time to finish what we've started," he whispered, his breath warm against her lips.

Lila's heart thudded as his fingers slowly entwined in her hair, bringing her closer. At last, with a slow smile, his mouth came down on hers. Her lips softened instinctively, moulding to his, and as his kiss deepened, she knew she had never been happier.

When they broke apart, Lila sighed and laid her head on his shoulder.

"Worth waiting for?" he whispered in her ear.

Lila breathed him in, his wide shoulders, his solid bulk. "Definitely," she whispered back.

They swayed dreamily, the music as soft and lilting as a breeze. Lila felt as if they were the only people in the room. Opening her eyes, her half-focused gaze settled on a familiar figure leaning against the wall on the far side of the room, a drink in his hand.

Josh was here. This wasn't Josh's kind of party – was it? She didn't even know he'd been invited. She realized with a strange lurch in her stomach that he was staring right at her. Even from this distance, there was something sad in his eyes as he watched the way she was moving around the dance floor in Ollie's arms.

Lila pulled her gaze away and buried her face against Ollie's jacket again. She felt weirdly guilty. A question flickered around the edges of her mind. She didn't want to ask it. But somehow it crept out of her mouth.

"Ollie?"

"Hmm?"

"Tell me honestly. Did you write to me?"

"Write to you when?"

"Was it you who wrote those notes I got in school?" She glanced at Josh again, but he was looking at the floor, swirling his drink thoughtfully in his hand. "I asked you, that afternoon on the beach when we nearly. . . You didn't actually answer my question, now I think about it. Are you my secret admirer, or not?"

"There's nothing secret about my admiration for you," he replied, stroking his thumb down her cheek.

His other hand cupped her face and his lips sought hers again. She kissed him back, but over Ollie's shoulder she was uncomfortably aware of the hurt on Josh's face as he set down his glass and disappeared into the crowd.

Ollie hadn't been her secret admirer after all.

TWENTY-FOUR

"What are you thinking?" Ollie asked as they danced around the floor, dappled with pink light from the spinning glitterball.

Lila had a hundred thoughts tumbling around in her head. "Nothing," she lied. It was far too complicated to explain.

"Are you bothered about the secret admirer thing?" he asked curiously.

The second lie of the night came to her lips. "No."

"It was probably a joke anyway," he went on easily. "I wouldn't worry about it. How many notes did you get?"

The thought that the notes might have been a joke cut Lila to the heart.

"A couple," she said shortly. "I thought they were very sweet."

"Don't be angry," Ollie said, lifting her chin so their eyes met. "Forget I said that," he amended with a grin. "You look even prettier with those sparks of fire in your eyes."

Lila gave a half-smile. They danced some more, and she tried to enjoy the feel of Ollie's arms around her waist. When the song finished and something livelier took over, she detached herself.

"I'm going to find a drink. Do you want anything?"

Ollie shook his head, and started dancing with Max. Feeling suddenly cold outside the warm circle of his arms, Lila made her way through the packed dance floor in search of Josh.

How could she have been so blind? It seemed obvious now she thought about it. Who, apart from Ollie and Polly, had bothered being nice to her in those early days? She needed to find him.

After fetching a couple of drinks, she hunted high and low for Josh's lanky frame, steering well clear of Eve holding court in the middle of the room. He had been wearing a dark jacket, which wasn't exactly easy to spot in the crowd.

Maybe he'd left. She winced as she remembered how she had been with Santiago that night on the beach, when she thought she had seen someone on the path to the secret cove. . . And tonight, she was clearly with Ollie. She had never given Josh a chance.

She found him at last, outside on the balcony at the back of the house. Candles lit the tables, and swags of pink lights garlanded the wrought iron railings. He was alone, the collar of his jacket turned up against the chill of the night, gazing absently down at the long flare-lit garden.

"Hey," Lila said hesitantly to his back.

Josh swung round. His cheeks coloured. "Oh. Hi."

She raised the two glasses of punch in his direction. "You want one of these?"

He took the drink silently. His jacket suited him, Lila thought, hanging long and sleek on his tall frame.

"So," she said, casting around for a good way to start this conversation. "Having a good time?"

"Sure," he said. "Standing around, talking to no one, not dancing. It's my kind of evening."

"Don't you like dancing?"

"It's more a case of dancing not liking *me*," he said drily. "One minute I have two perfectly normal feet. The next minute, they've both turned left on me."

The garden below was dotted with pale figures hurrying among the trees, giggling, holding hands and kissing. It felt a little weird standing here watching them, Lila thought.

"Where's Ollie then?" Josh asked, sipping his drink.

Lila steeled herself. *I know I'm right*, she thought. *All I have to do is ask.*

"Let's not talk about Ollie," she said. "I have a question to ask you."

"If it's about the Berlin Airlift, go right ahead," he said. "If it's about something else, I reserve the right not to answer."

"Did you write me those letters?"

Lila watched as his drink shook a little in his hand.

"What letters?"

It was true. Lila knew it as surely as she knew anything.

"The letters that kept me sane in the first few days

at Heartside High," she answered, putting her hand on his without thinking.

He pulled his hand away clumsily, and then pushed his glasses up his nose. "I know you're with Ollie. And anyway, I wouldn't mess up our friendship with any sad attempts at romance. I mean, look at you. The fact that you even talk to me is a miracle. Girls as pretty as you don't usually bother. Why would I write you letters?"

He thinks I'm pretty, Lila thought. The realization made her flush. She remembered the drawing he had done in his sketchbook, in their first history class together. Sweet, lovely Josh.

"I loved them," she said honestly.

He gave half a smile. "Then the letter-writer got one thing right at least. Whoever he was."

The French windows behind them banged hard against the wall.

"There you are!" Rhi laughed, her arms slung round Eve and Polly. "We've been looking everywhere for you. Come on, it's nearly the last dance."

Polly seized Lila by the hand. "Come on," she insisted. "I've lost Flynn and I need a dance partner. Last chance!"

Lila glanced round for Josh. But he had slid away

as usual, tall and ghost-like. Would she ever solve the puzzle that was Josh Taylor?

She let herself be dragged back to the dance floor, where Polly started jumping around while Rhi and Eve swayed elegantly and perfectly in time with the tune. Letting her arms float above her head, Lila lost herself in the music again. Ollie was messing around at the front with Max, she noticed. She couldn't help smiling.

"Ollie's dancing is insane," Polly giggled as they danced. "He should stick to football."

"Max isn't much better," Rhi grinned.

They all watched as Max ran across the floor, Ollie hot on his heels.

"I forgot to tell you, Lila," said Eve. "Your dress really is gorgeous."

"Thanks," said Lila in surprise. "So's yours."

Eve was nearly impossible to predict, she thought.

"This is such a perfect party," Rhi said exultantly. "Great music, great fun, and everyone's getting on really well at last."

Polly whooped and danced a bit harder. Laughing, Eve joined in, losing some of her elegance as the music pumped harder in her blood. Lila allowed herself to relax, and look around, and really enjoy herself. Rhi was right. It had truly been an excellent party.

The song ended, and the telltale sound of another slow dance started up. Eve pulled Lila into a sudden hug. Rhi smiled broadly at the sight, and spun around on the spot with her arms stretched up high and her eyes closed.

"You may have won the battle for Ollie," Eve whispered, tightening her grip around Lila's shoulders, "but I'll win the war. Keep watching your back, new girl. If you thought it was bad before, you haven't seen anything yet."

She planted a loud kiss on Lila's frozen cheek. "It's been so much fun having you here," she said with her hostess smile fixed firmly back on her flawless face. "I can't wait to know you better."

"Finally," said Rhi, watching Eve drift off the dance floor. "I can't tell you how great it feels to see you guys getting along at last."

Polly went to fetch a drink as Max wandered over to claim Rhi for the slow dance. Lila discovered that she couldn't move her feet. Eve had just taken things to a whole new level.

"Hey, beautiful," said Ollie, catching her round the waist and spinning her to face him. "I love this song. I'm so glad I can dance it with you."

She let Ollie pull her in his arms. She turned her face up to his, and was rewarded with a deep and heady kiss that she felt right down to her toes.

I'll forget about that look on Josh's face when he saw me with Ollie, she vowed to herself breathlessly, twisting her hands through Ollie's hair and moulding herself to his swaying body in the glittering party light. *I'll forget about Eve. I'll forget about everything but this kiss, right here and right now.*

Eve Somerstown could bring it on. Lila had the hottest guy in school, and good friends around her.

If Eve wanted war, she'd give her war.

Maybe it was time for a new queen bee in Heartside.

The story continues. . .
Read the opening of the next book:
The Trouble With Love

Polly Nelson couldn't take her eyes off the stitching along the hem of the flowy skirt she was wearing. She had chosen it so carefully that afternoon. She couldn't believe she'd left the house in something that looked so bad.

The campfire crackled merrily, the smell of toasting marshmallows mingling with the salty beach air, the pumping bass from Max's MP3 and the lively sound of chatter. It was surprisingly warm for a February afternoon, even without the fire. Polly tucked the offending skirt under her legs, hoping that she wouldn't think about it so much that way. She looked terrible. She hoped no one would notice.

On the opposite side of the fire, Polly's best friend Lila Murray had finished threading her stick with marshmallows and was placing them in the flames. Her glossy brown hair was whipped up by the wind coming in from the sea, and she was laughing at something her boyfriend Ollie Wright was saying. She was so pretty, Polly thought, and had such infectious enthusiasm for everything. No wonder Ollie was mad about her. It was hard to believe Lila had only come to Heartside Bay a few weeks ago. It felt like they'd known each other for half their lives.

It's half-term, Polly scolded herself. *You're in the secret cove with your friends, a bonfire, marshmallows and great music. What's not to like?*

This skirt looks awful, her thoughts replied at once.

What are you going to do about it? Polly challenged herself. *Take it off and dance around the beach in your underwear?*

Her gaze flickered towards Ollie. He looked extra-gorgeous when he laughed, she thought wistfully.

She'd had a secret crush on Ollie since her first day at Heartside High. He had dropped a pencil by her feet in Year Eight, and she had kept it. She had written in detail about him in her diary in Year Nine, and treasured every private conversation they had ever had. After all these years, she still couldn't stop her heart from fluttering every time she saw him. And now he was Lila's.

As she gazed at Ollie, Polly caught Lila's eye. She instantly felt guilty. Did the fact that she fancied her best friend's boyfriend show in her face? Her wide hazel eyes were much too expressive, she knew. She loosed her hair and let it swing round her face like a thick black curtain.

"Half-term at last," Lila sighed happily. She fiddled with her marshmallow stick. "I can't believe it's here. We're going to have *so* much fun."

Polly felt a wave of relief. Lila hadn't read anything in her expression. It looked like her complicated feelings for Ollie were still a secret.

Ollie dusted sand off his jeans and snuggled his arm round Lila's shoulders. "And it starts right here," he said. "Are my marshmallows done yet?"

Lila guarded her marshmallow stick, baring her teeth like a dog. "Cook your own!" she warned, smiling.

"What's yours is mine," Ollie said innocently. "That's the way relationships work."

Lila kicked him with one bare, sandy foot. "You wish!"

Ollie launched himself at Lila, tickling her until she begged, squealing, for mercy. Then he cut off her laughter with a kiss.

Polly suddenly felt more lonely than she'd ever felt in her life.

"I'm going for a paddle," she said, getting up.

"Want some company?" Lila said, pushing Ollie off and raising herself up on her elbows. The sand in her hair made her look like an off-duty mermaid.

Polly shook her head. "Save a marshmallow for me?"

"Of course, Pol," Lila said warmly.

"Hey!" Ollie said in a mock-indignant voice. "You're letting her have one, but not me?"

Lila and Ollie were the perfect couple, Polly thought with a sigh as she took off her shoes and moved away from the campfire. They were both gorgeous, and bubbly, and popular. It had taken Lila a few weeks to settle in to her new school – thanks mainly to queen bee Eve Somerstown causing trouble – but now she was in the middle of every social event in Heartside and almost more popular than Eve herself. Lila had long legs, a rich laugh and beautiful thick brown hair. Why would Ollie look at anyone else – least of all, Polly?

Enough with this obsession, she thought, straightening her shoulders. It was time to move on. Anyway, Ollie represented everything she despised in boys. Dumb sexist humour, never taking anything seriously, and only ever thinking about football. He was wrong for her in every way.

There must be someone better out there for you, she consoled herself. *Someone more intelligent than Ollie, more sensitive, less sporty. Maybe someone with deep political convictions. Now that would be a dream boy.*

She reached the edge of the sea and let the cold waves swish over her toes. The sea always calmed her down and helped her to think more clearly. She couldn't imagine living inland. It would be torture, knowing that the ocean was curling and crashing over someone else's feet, not her own.

Polly glanced over her shoulder at the sound of laughter. Rhi and Eve were chasing Rhi's boyfriend Max down the beach, throwing handfuls of sand after him. Max ran backwards, grinning and waving as Rhi and Eve chased him. His dark curly hair blew around his head.

"Catch me if you can!" he whooped teasingly.

"Oh, we'll catch you!" Eve shouted. "Don't worry about that, Max!"

"No one eats our marshmallows and gets away with it!" Rhi added, gasping with laughter as she flung her sand in Max's direction. It fell harmlessly by his feet.

"Typical girl," Max taunted with a grin, racing back towards the campfire. "Can't throw to save your life!"

Why can't I be more like Eve? Polly thought, watching them. *Totally comfortable hanging out with her best friend and her boyfriend?*

She shook her head, surprised at herself. She could never be like Eve in any way. Eve made everyone's lives a misery. Lila had been through hell in her first couple of weeks at Heartside High because of Eve. She had made Polly's life miserable too. Eve was as trustworthy as a snake.

Polly watched as Eve, true to form, threw herself beside the others by the campfire, accidentally on purpose knocking Lila's arm and spilling her water in her lap.

"Whoops," she drawled, not sounding the least bit sorry.

"Whoops yourself," Lila said, and dumped what was left of her water over Eve's head.

"Ugh!"

Eve jumped furiously to her feet, mopping hard at her cashmere jumper. Rhi helped her to mop off the worst of the water with Max's help. Ollie just laughed.

"I'm really sorry, Eve," said Lila with an innocent-looking shrug. "It was a total mistake. My hand has a life of its own, didn't you know?"

Even from a distance, Polly could see Eve's eyes were glittering with rage.

"That wasn't kind, Lila," said Rhi reproachfully.

"She did it to me first," Lila pointed out, mopping herself dry. "You have to learn to take what you dish out, Eve. Just be glad I wasn't drinking anything sticky."

"I spilled your drink by *accident*," Eve hissed.

"Funny kind of accident," said Lila, rolling her eyes. "You have to stop with all these silly games, Eve. We're all tired of your behaviour."

"Give it a rest, will you?" said Max lazily, swiping a marshmallow. "This is supposed to be a party."

"I will not," Eve snapped, and jumped to her feet. "She started it."

Several of the other girls in their class rallied round Eve with Rhi and Max. Lila stood up warily, with Ollie, a group of Ollie's footballing mates and a bunch of other kids clustered round her in support.

Polly felt nervous. Things had been extra tense between Lila and Eve since Valentine's Day. It was great that Lila wasn't putting up with Eve's tricks any more, but things were getting out of hand.

It was beginning to feel like the whole school was split between supporters of Eve and supporters of Lila. The tension was awful. It wasn't the best way to start half-term.

"Fight!" someone yelled.

Continued. . .